I lost my heart to him before the hull grated against the sand. All at once I understood how Penelope could have left me to follow Odysseus anywhere on earth, and I forgave her for it.

Hessia would say I was bewitched by Aphrodite, struck by one of her invisible love arrows. If this sudden passion was Aphrodite's doing, I forgave her too.

He leaped from the ship and bounded up the beach to embrace Menelaus at the water's edge. Afterward he walked toward me, smiling a secret smile as if conscious of his heart-stopping grace. It was a joy to watch him move.

I don't remember if I managed to say anything. He took my hand, his fingers warm, his eyes a blazing blue. "Helen, your beauty is for immortals to describe. For once in my life I'm speechless."

—from *Inside the Walls of Troy*

Clemence McLaren lives in Hawaii, where she works as a teacher. *Inside the Walls of Troy* is her first novel.

INSIDE THE WALLS OF TROY

OF TROY

A Novel of the Women Who Lived
the Trojan War

CLEMENCE McLAREN

LAUREL-LEAF
BOOKS

Published by
Dell Laurel-Leaf
an imprint of
Random House Children's Books
a division of Random House, Inc.
1540 Broadway
New York, New York 10036

Visit us on the Web! www.randomhouse.com/teens

Educators and librarians, for a variety of teaching tools, visit us at www.randomhouse.com/teachers

ISBN: 0-440-22749-6

RL: 5.6

Reprinted by arrangement with Atheneum Publishers

Printed in the United States of America

September 1998

10 9 8 7

OPM

To my mother, Grayce Lilian Berg

Contents

PART ONE

HELEN'S STORY

CHAPTER ONE

~•~

Because of my extraordinary beauty, they say a thousand ships were launched, fifty thousand men died, and the world's greatest city fell to dust. They say great Zeus himself was my father, that the gods never sculpted a more perfect face than mine. But behind that face was a girl named Helen, who loved horses, played the flute, bit her nails. This is her story—my story.

I was twelve years old the day my childhood ended. My cousin Penelope and I were playing knucklebones in the women's quarters, the shutters closed against the endless heat of the summer afternoon. Outside, locusts shrilled their song into the stillness. I was gloating because I had just thrown the tiny bones, carved from the joints of mountain deer, and caught a record four on the back of my hand.

Penelope shook her head. "You're cheating again, Helen," she said wearily. "You know you're supposed to toss them as high as your eyes." She was fifteen and had recently given up games for the serious business of getting

~ 3 ~

ready for marriage. She was only playing knucklebones to be nice to me, and I resented it.

"I *did*! You weren't watching! Never mind, I quit." I threw the bones into her lap.

"Where are you going?"

"Down to the stables to look at the new foal. I think I'll call him Thunder. . . ."

"Not without a veil. Or get one of the slaves to follow you with a sunscreen. You'd be brown as a peasant if you had your way, running around with the horses."

There was a time, not very long ago, when my cousin would have run around with me and not worried about her complexion. "Only fifteen and talking like an old married lady. Who put you in charge of me anyway?" I snapped.

But Penelope refused to get angry. She sighed in her new, grown-up way. "You can't be the most beautiful girl in all of Greece with a sunburned nose."

"I don't care about my nose! And I don't want a slave following me around."

"Then I'm calling Nurse. She'll make you behave. . . ."

But she didn't need to call. At that moment the door flew open, smashing against the wall, and our nurse, Hessia, ran into the room. "*Pirates!*" she screamed. "They've broken into the citadel!" Her round body shook with fear. "They say it's Theseus, the Athenian!"

Penelope jumped to her feet, the knucklebones clattering to the marble floor. "Are they stealing sheep and cattle?"

"No, they were spotted on the trail riding straight through. They've killed the gate guards!"

"Then they must be after Helen. They've heard the stories. . . ." Color drained from my cousin's face as she surveyed the room. We heard faint shouting, muffled by the locusts' continuous screech.

Hessia stood tearing at her sparse gray hair. "Immortal Gods! With all the men at the hunt and no one to protect us but house slaves!"

"Draw the bolts, good Hessia. We'll have to hide her in here," Penelope said. "Come, Helen, under the bed. We'll roll you in one of the fleece rugs and pack the others around you. Come on! Be brave."

But I was frozen with fear. I heard the crash of the great portals that opened into the main court and felt Penelope grip my arms and lift me from the floor.

Tucked against the wall under the bed, my heart thudding inside my rib cage, I thought I would surely suffocate. But the worst part was not being able to see what was happening. Was it really *Theseus*? In his youth he had killed the Minotaur, the monster bull of Crete. He had become king of Athens. But the gods had sent him bad luck in recent years, and he had turned to piracy. He had raided our coasts twice. The last time, he carried off my father's prize stallion. This time the prize was me.

"Penelope, I'm afraid!" I sniffled into the fleece.

"Hush now. I'm going to pretend Nurse is dying. She looks pale as death; maybe they'll believe us."

The mattress sagged and pressed me into the stone floor as Nurse stretched out above me with a convincing groan.

"Penelope, I can't *breathe*!"

A terrifying noise of shattering wood filled the room, then a high-pitched wail from Hessia, followed by Penelope's outraged voice—"You disturb the dying moments of our faithful servant"—then silence and the shuffle of feet.

I wanted to scream out and end the awful waiting. At last I heard a male voice reporting, in the clipped accents of the North, that the cupboard was empty.

"Look under the bed then," said a deeper voice, accustomed to command.

"Lord Theseus, I was told you were a gentleman. . . ." Penelope's voice sounded almost normal.

"A gentleman, my clever maid, but not a fool."

Rough hands grabbed hold of my ankle, and I screamed. They pulled the fleece from under the bed and rolled me out at his feet, a tall, brawny man, built like a god, with curly gray hair and beard. He stood legs apart, arms crossed, eyes twinkling with cruel humor.

I think it was this amusement that forced me, all at once, to pretend to be brave. If Penelope could face him with dignity, so could I. "Welcome to Sparta, King Theseus," I said, scrambling to my feet. "You *are* King Theseus?"

He threw back his head and laughed. "I am! And you have a novel way of welcoming travelers to your court, Helen of the Flaxen Hair. The stories have not exaggerated; it's an extraordinary color. Turn around."

"Stand still, Helen," said Penelope, moving in between us. "Lord Theseus, we offer our apologies. My uncle and his sons are off hunting. They are due back any moment. . . ."

Theseus smiled down at my cousin, at the coiled ebony hair, the dark eyes full of wisdom beyond her years. "And you must be Lady Penelope, another beauty. Too bad I can't take you both. But I need someone to deliver my message. Besides, your uncle Tyndareus and his illustrious sons—who have had the bad judgment to leave this golden princess with only four gate guards—will pay a king's ransom for *her!*" With that, he picked me up and threw me over his shoulder.

"But she's only a child!"

"She's past twelve. Every warrior in Greece has heard stories of her!"

"You'll pay for this!"

"It is Tyndareus, her father, who will pay—her weight in gold! And so that her honor and chances for marriage are protected, we'll take your servingwoman as well." He bowed toward the couch. "If she would get up from her deathbed and accompany us to the horses."

Penelope ran after our strange procession all the way to the citadel gates. In the lead was Theseus, with me dangling from his shoulder, followed by his five warriors, and then Hessia, who was alternately weeping, invoking the gods, and insulting the house slaves for their failure to come to our rescue, yelling accusations like, "You there, Naxos, you craven coward, I see you cringing behind the chamber pots!"

Hanging from Theseus' iron-muscled shoulder, jolted by each of his giant strides, I began to feel light-headed. None of it seemed real.

"Wait, she needs a cloak for the night's chill, and a veil to protect her from the sun. . . ." Penelope's voice finally broke. "It is *indecent* for her to appear outside the palace unveiled!"

"We'll steal them on our way down to the port!" Theseus laughed. "And in Athens she can have a whole new wardrobe! I'll add it to your bill."

I was being abducted by pirates and my cousin was still worrying about my complexion. "Penelope!" I shouted back. "Take care of my foal!"

CHAPTER TWO

❧❧

N o one spoke on the ride down the steep, winding trail to the sea. The men communicated in a language of grunts, and Hessia, to judge from her bright red cheeks, was too overcome with heat to keep up her accusations. After a while I stopped crying and stopped praying for help—my father and brothers weren't going to return from the hunt until after dark.

There was nothing in the world but the heat and the dust crunching between my teeth. I should have listened to Penelope. A veil would have soaked up the rivulets of perspiration now burning my eyes. My robe stuck to my back and my knees slipped on the flanks of the bay mare each time she shifted her weight down the inclines of polished rock.

Theseus had rounded up the horses, a sorry lot, before coming up the mountain to the citadel. But during our four-hour descent he found nothing left to steal. Our villagers had fled, taking their meager belongings with them. Under the sun's white glare their beehive-shaped huts looked as if they had never been occupied.

The forty oarsmen on board Theseus' long ship, *Minotaur*, named for the monster bull from Crete, had watched our progress down the mountain. They sat poised at the oarlocks ready for a quick departure—and staring at me in a way that made me conscious of my sweat-soaked robe.

After he lifted me on board, Theseus yelled at the mate to cast off the hawsers, then yelled for a cloak to cover me. A galley slave came running with one of yellow linen that must have belonged to Theseus. Hessia, breathing heavily, made an effort to arrange it around my shoulders.

"My nurse needs water," I told Theseus, who stopped shouting at the crew and looked down at me.

"We all need water. And you are not in a position to issue orders. . . ."

Hessia pawed at my hands. "Don't antagonize them; they'll slit our throats."

"Not likely. I'm worth nothing with a slit throat. And you're here to ensure my virtue. He'd have to deduct at least fifty talents of gold from the ransom if he let you die."

"Women on board, yapping like puppies." Theseus snorted. "Mikon, bring water and some figs! Over here!" But in spite of his gruff voice, his eyes held a twinkle of mirth.

That flyspecked water was as delicious as anything I'd ever tasted, but I had no stomach for the figs. My burst of anger had exhausted me. I dropped down beside Hessia on the dirty deck boards, hugging the yellow cloak around me. I think they could have thrown me overboard at that moment and I would not have had the energy to care.

The rowing captain began his chant:

> *"One for Poseidon, Lord of the Sea,*
>   *Two for our king and state,*
>   *Three for the Nereids, swimming free . . ."*

The oarsmen strained in unison, and the *Minotaur* pulled away from the coasts of my ancestors. I thought of my bed back home, the smooth sheets that smelled of the lavender that Penelope folded inside them in the storage cupboard. Was Penelope crying over me? I wondered. Probably not, not in public anyway. She was more likely coordinating the ransom effort in her quiet way, listening to my father and brothers rant and then suggesting what treasures we might part with to accumulate the necessary gold. "They *will* pay the ransom," I told myself. "They have to!" My face ached with the effort of holding my mouth in a brave line.

Two slaves arrived with fleece rugs and blankets. Another brought a basin of water. Hessia, too tired to wash, crawled into her bedroll, moaning softly. I was splashing water on my face when Theseus himself came with a jug of honeyed wine and a two-handled cup.

"Swig it down, there's a good girl," he said.

I obeyed, eyes brimming with foolish tears. I thought he would laugh at me, but he didn't. With a grave expression he took the empty cup from my hands. "We may look like cutthroats and scoundrels, but these men consider it the greatest of honors to have you on board, daughter of Zeus Almighty. No one will harm you. The gods who rule the wide heavens watch over their own."

"That's servant gossip. My father is Tyndareus, king of Sparta." I wiped my eyes with the back of my hand.

"We can argue your parentage in the morning," he said,

smiling. "For now, forget everything and let Hypnos take you on a dream journey."

I watched him climb down into the hull to supervise the hoisting of the mast. I remembered stories of how, as a very young man, he became a hero to all the young people in Greece when he killed the Cretan Minotaur, the half man, half bull that demanded its awful diet of young victims every spring. Some villages still held festivals in his honor.

The crew strapped on the square sail, and it bellied out with a southwest wind, as if the gods approved our destination. The rocky coast lay empty of rescuers, empty of life.

I stretched out on my purple blanket and looked up at the twilight sky. After the heat of the day the evening was soft as a caress. I felt in my body the motion of the ship, taking me on the sea's broad back away from home. The sky faded from blue at the top of the vault through all the shades of violet to deep rose at the horizon.

Sea and sky met in perfect calm, yet my heart continued to race as I pondered the possibilities for rescue. I knew my brothers well enough to judge how this kidnapping would assault their pride. I knew how starved they were for battle. If Sparta went to war over my kidnapping, what would happen to *me*? Would Theseus be true to his word that we would not be harmed?

It was dawn before I finally drifted into sleep, and then I dreamed I was a Nereid, handmaiden to Poseidon, swimming through blue-green grottos, chased by an enormous fish with sharp, curving teeth. I awoke to hear my nurse complaining about the hard deck. "Sleeping on the floor. Like house slaves," she was telling poor Mikon. "My lady needs a proper bed. Look at the poor love!"

Later that morning, refreshed with pickled eggs and barley meal and apparently convinced they weren't going to slit our throats, Hessia became her bossy self again. As we sailed down the coast, she badgered the crew about their bad manners, their crude language, and their staring. "She's a *princess*, you oafs, destined for one of your betters. Keep your filthy eyes off her!"

I think they enjoyed her harangues. They exchanged bawdy insults with her in their clipped northern accents, but were strangely shy with me. By the time we reached the southern islands, the men were calling her Auntie.

I sat in silence, hugging my knees and looking up at the rocky seascapes, still worrying about a war. How could my beauty be a gift of the gods if it would cause men to die for me? I wondered which warriors and even which horses would perish if Sparta attacked Athens. Our horses need to be trained for battle; otherwise they will panic and throw their riders when they hear the clash of swords or the screams of the wounded, or when they step on the bodies littering the field.

I found myself estimating which horses would be selected for such training. Several times Theseus came over to where I sat, and I swallowed down my tears. Once he reached down and patted my shoulder, then shook his head and stomped off.

Hessia said, "He's worried about you, sitting here pining."

"Of course he's worried. I'm worth at least a hundred talents of gold to him."

She clucked her tongue. "He has a soft spot for you, mark my words."

After a moment I said, "What if my father and brothers wage war instead of ransoming me?"

"They wouldn't dare. Not against the walled citadel of Athens! All the world has heard of it, built on a great hill that rises like magic in the middle of the plain. No army has ever scaled it. Look! Out there! Dolphins in our wake! A good omen."

Hessia would never have admitted it, but the kidnapping had become a holiday, the only one she'd ever known. By the second day she was calling Theseus "my lord," and he had begun to refer to her as "the crone," affectionately. Even I could not deny his innate nobility, and Hessia was old enough to remember him as the hero he'd once been, the tall, bronzed slayer of monsters. In her eyes the old pirate had become a gentleman.

CHAPTER THREE

❧

On the third day I continued to brood over our future, painting mental pictures of bloody battles fought in the name of Helen. Eventually, though, as we rounded the southern cape, and the wind pushed our painted galley out into open seas, I began to look with wonder at the new surroundings. I had never sailed beyond the southern islands. The world continued on forever, it seemed.

At sunset Theseus came and sat beside me on deck, pointing out towns along the Peloponnisos Peninsula where he and his best friend, Pirithous, had shared adventures.

This Pirithous, according to Hessia, stood almost as tall as Theseus, and was every bit as dashing. She'd learned from the crew that this wild warrior from the slopes of Mount Olympus was the reason we were here on board the *Minotaur*. Always in competition, he and Theseus had boasted that they would each kidnap a daughter of Zeus, and it was rumored that Zeus was my real father, not Tyndareus of Sparta. The greatest of all the gods, forger of lightning bolts, had supposedly disguised himself as a white swan and made love to Leda, my beautiful mother. She tried to resist him, but not very successfully, because soon afterward she gave birth to two large eggs from which my twin brothers Castor and Polydeuces and I were hatched. Or so the stories went.

The fact that my twin brothers and I were blond in a typically Greek family of olive-skinned brunettes helped support these rumors of miraculous birth. The Greeks have always made much of fair hair; it's a novelty in our land. When my brothers and I were babies, peasants lined up on sacrifice days for a chance to touch our curls. They considered it good luck.

Our mother died when we were very young. The servants continued to whisper about our parentage and called my brothers "the heavenly twins," which made them both unbearably arrogant. Later, stories began to spread about my divine beauty. I asked Hessia about them, but she only said, "Servants' gossip not fit for the ears of young ladies."

But Theseus had promised to discuss my parentage. It was the afternoon of the fifth day when I worked up the courage to ask him. Hessia, who would have put an end to such questioning, was off swapping stories with the oarsmen. Theseus stood beside me on deck, describing with wild gestures a skirmish he'd fought years before on the opposite coast, near the Gulf of Tiryns. He and Pirithous had been ambushed by Phoenician pirates.

"Was I really fathered by Zeus?" I interrupted.

"What disrespect is this? And here I am telling of Pirithous's slashing blow!" He smiled down at me then. "Have you looked at yourself, girl? You'll find real mirrors in the palace at Athens, not those warped sheets of bronze you have in Sparta. When we arrive, you'll have a look at yourself."

"What for?"

He snorted his impatience. "Because your beauty surpasses that of mortal women. *That's* why all the kings in the Greek world will be fighting to have you. You've probably heard *I* was sired by Poseidon," he added with a shrug of modesty. "My own beauty has been somewhat tarnished by the years, but in my prime . . ."

"But how could he have *done* it? I mean, Zeus, in the body of a swan, and my mother . . . fighting him? How did he manage it?"

I think my question embarrassed him. "I'm not going to explain that . . . business." He frowned down at the deck. "But I wouldn't believe everything I heard about Zeus assuming those disguises—swans and bulls and the like—in order to get close to women before they ran away. Think about it. If you were an ordinary mortal woman and Zeus appeared to you in all his glory, would *you* run away?" He leaned closer and whispered, "Or would you need an excuse for your ordinary mortal husband when you were simply . . . overwhelmed." He fluttered his hands helplessly.

I laughed at his portrayal of helplessness. But it was still impossible to think of myself as daughter of the most powerful member of the Olympian family, Father Zeus, the Thunder King.

Often in the week that followed, Theseus found time to answer my questions about the wide world outside Sparta. His voice softened each time he pointed out places where he had fought or offered sacrifices with his former queen, Hippolyta. Everyone in Greece knew their love story. He had stolen her from her northern tribe of Amazons, fierce women warriors, and she devoted herself to him for the rest of her life.

She was a better fighter than most men, and a woman of startling golden beauty. When Athens was attacked by tribes from the North, among them her own people, she had thrown herself in front of Theseus and caught in her own breast an arrow meant for him. His rage over her death enabled him to clear his land of invaders almost single-handedly.

Hessia said Theseus kept her rooms at the palace exactly as she left them when she went off to that final battle, her cloak thrown across the bed, her silver comb with strands of pale gold in its teeth. Hessia thought I reminded him of her, that with my fair hair, I could have been the daughter they never had.

Theseus did seem to enjoy my company. He was the first adult who had ever really talked to me, other than Hessia, of course, whose talking was more often a curse than a blessing. In those final days I found myself wishing the voyage wouldn't end.

The sprawling port city of Piraeus was the ultimate wonder. I could have stood for hours and watched the rivers of people.

"See, over there?" Theseus said, pointing at three men with long swishing robes, white turbans, and blue-black faces.

"Have they painted themselves?" I asked.

He laughed at my ignorance. "They're Ethiopians, from Africa, which lies at the edge of the world. The sun has burned them that color."

"I never imagined the gods fashioned men in so many colors. Look, there's another one!"

The narrow streets teemed with people, yellow-haired Thracians, red-bearded Macedonians, blue-black Africans among the dark-haired Greeks and darker Asians. The air was charged with their energy.

For my trip uphill to the great rock fortress the Athenians call the Acropolis, I rode behind Theseus in his bronze chariot, pulled by four perfectly matched black horses, as peasants scrambled for a place at the front, and children were held aloft.

Theseus provided a white cloak trimmed in silver embroidery and a matching veil, which hung down over my eyebrows in the Athenian fashion. I was grateful for the privacy it provided, for just as I was staring into the faces of the crowd, they were lining the road, calling my name in a medley of strange accents.

"Whatever do they *want*?" I shouted into his ear.

"To tell their grandchildren they saw Helen of the Flaxen Hair! That they touched the hem of her robe . . ." He cursed as a man leaped up toward me and fell back into a scramble of hands.

"But *why*?"

"Because you're *Helen*, the most beautiful woman the world will ever know."

I couldn't have guessed that my beauty would also make me one of the most despised. Still, in the full sun of midday, I felt a shiver of fear.

CHAPTER FOUR

The Acropolis shimmered in the mist as if suspended in space, more magnificent than anything I could have imagined. Hessia was right. It was magic the way the huge flat rock rose from the sloping plain. No enemy could ever scale the walls to attack the white marble citadel perched on top.

The women's quarters alone were larger than our entire palace back in Sparta. Silken curtains drifted in the breeze; marble floors mirrored the shimmer of fine robes. Unlike the crowds along the road, the Athenian servants were too well-bred to stare when Theseus handed me over to them. They acted as if receiving stolen princesses were a routine task. After the briefest welcome a tall woman with coiled silver hair signaled for two slaves, who undressed me and helped me into a deep bath. I pointed toward Hessia, standing awkwardly in the corner. "My nurse," I said. "She usually takes care of me."

The silver-haired lady glanced at Hessia. "These slaves, from the island of Scyros, have the softest hands in all the world. They're trained from birth in the art of the bath," she said, picking up my robe and discarding it in a basket with a look of distaste. "Your woman can stay and watch. I daresay she won't recognize you when we've finished."

I had never seen such a large tub. Hot water actually flowed through pipes into the palace. Spigots in the shape of lions' heads projected a fine spray down upon the bather. The soft-handed slaves massaged peach-pit oil into my skin and then scraped it off with an ivory scraper. Rose petals floated in the sun-shot water; I cupped them in my hands and buried my face in their fragrance. It felt heavenly to be wet and clean, although I wished the ladies would say something. I missed the easy chatter of our servants back home.

Afterward they rubbed my skin with more precious oils and perfumed my hair. Even Hessia knew enough to sit quietly in a corner and watch their progress, once or twice telling me needlessly to hold still, as if I would have dared fidget under their skilled hands.

Standing before these frowning strangers, I felt like a prize heifer being readied for the altar. Yet there was an excitement about it too. I kept wishing for the mirror Theseus had promised so I could see myself in the robes they slipped over my head.

The silver-haired woman was difficult to satisfy. After rejecting the first six, she sent one of the slaves to the storeroom for still another stack of richly embroidered robes, in layers of azure and vermillion and palest mauve.

The one they finally selected was made of layered semi-sheer panels in blue and green, the color constantly changing, like the sea in the filtered light of clouds. Small iron weights were sewn into the corners at the neckline to keep the silky fabric from slipping off at the shoulders. They fastened a silver girdle around my waist and arranged the folds with expert hands. Then they plaited my hair in a coil and finally led me through endless corridors to the king's apartments.

Theseus nodded approval, dismissing them with a wave of his fingers. Holding my shoulders, he positioned me in front of a floor-length looking glass of extraordinary clarity. He said, "See for yourself why they would risk death just to touch the hem of your robe."

I saw a golden braid framing my forehead, blue eyes, a slender neck.

"Daughter of Zeus, you are a treasure more precious than gold, because your beauty will not last for centuries. It is a prize that must be possessed now, in the pulsebeat of one mortal lifetime. Soon every warrior in Greece will be fighting to possess it. If I were ten years younger, I'd be fighting myself!"

Silence hung over us as I studied the princess in the mirror, the last rays of the sun gilding her crown of braids. She didn't seem real. I was Helen of Sparta, who cheated at knucklebones and chased after my foal. The young woman in the mirror was an alien presence who seemed to demand something I would never be able to deliver.

"You're no longer a child," he finally said, as if reading my doubts. "You're a creature of legend, just as I have been, marked by the ancestry of the gods."

"You never felt afraid . . . of your destiny?"

"*Me?* I *chose* my destiny—surely you've heard the stories?—I picked the most dangerous route to claim my heritage in Athens. I went forward like a *man*—hrrrumph! Fortunately, no one is asking such a thing of you. You'll return to Sparta and marry a great king. Travelers will come from far away just to gawk at you. Like today."

"What if I'm not equal to it? What if he finds me boring, this great king? Surely beauty is not enough to please him."

Theseus gave his snort of impatience. "I'm not your nursemaid, girl! Get Hessia to teach you how to keep a man happy."

"Oh, she's explained about sex. And I know about running a fine household. . . . I mean, will his eyes soften when he speaks my name, the way yours do whenever you speak of Hippolyta? Will he love me?"

"Love is different from sex, but don't ask me to explain how. I'm just an old soldier. For that, you'll have to consult an oracle, and he'll talk nonsense." He left me staring into the mirror and stomped over to the open doors. "Come out to the garden; I've ordered almond pastries. They're nothing like the lumps of congealed dough that pass for sweets in your country. Thundering Zeus, how I've missed the refinements of home!"

Many, many times in the following weeks I went back to that looking glass, as if seeking the answer to some riddle I couldn't define. And I couldn't stop wondering about the mastery of Theseus' voice whenever he came up against a memory of his dead wife.

He never showed me her rooms, although I would have given anything to see them. On all other subjects he enjoyed presiding over my education, giving advice even about clothes and makeup. "A bit of kohl above the eyes is fine," he told me one afternoon. "Maybe a touch of alkanet juice on the cheeks. But don't let them talk you into putting white lead powder on your face. It will run if you shed a tear. A man doesn't want to see that."

He showed me how the Athenian women hold balls of amber in their hands to keep them cool. He gave me a flute and brought in a Thracian from the North to give me lessons. "It will be soothing for your husband if you play for him in the evenings."

Most lectures were about pleasing this future husband. According to Theseus, nothing worked better than a look of witless admiration. "It doesn't matter if our words are trite and our decisions downright foolish," he told me. "We all want to be admired."

I laughed at his demonstration of the proper witless expression. "I'll bet Hippolyta never looked at you like that," I said, and Theseus changed the subject. I couldn't imagine using this look on a husband without giggling. I couldn't wait to demonstrate it for Penelope.

Penelope. Each time I thought about my cousin, I felt a stab of guilt. She was probably sick with worry over me, while I was here in Athens wearing new robes, exploring the vast palace, laughing at silly jokes with Theseus. Penelope was made of stronger stuff; she would never have allowed herself to laugh with the enemy.

Not that they ever let me enjoy myself for very long. The fun always ended in lectures about this creature of legend I was about to become, like a perfect butterfly about to emerge from its cocoon.

"It's not ladylike to stuff yourself with pastries like that," Hessia reminded me one day, spoiling my enjoyment of the sticky almond sweets Theseus ordered every afternoon.

She never scolded me for licking honey off my fingers back home.

"She's just showing off," I told Theseus. "In Sparta, *everybody* licks their fingers." But for once he didn't make fun of our Spartan backwardness, a favorite joke among the Athenians.

"You also have to teach her not to plop herself into a chair," he told Hessia. "She needs to lower her behind—gracefully."

Hessia sat beaming and nodding, a perfect look of witless admiration on her puffy face. I got up and flounced toward the door, swishing the hem of my violet robe on the polished floor just as the Athenian ladies do.

"And one more thing," Theseus shouted after me. "You'll have to stop biting your nails!" I heard him ask Nurse, "Can't you dip her fingers in bitterroot?"

"They're *my* nails!" I shouted back. "I'll bite them if I want to!"

I sat on the citadel wall, hugging my knees and studying my unsightly nails and cuticles. Below me on the plain, cooking fires twinkled in the rosy dusk. Farmers were herding their flocks back to their villages.

Theseus had enlarged the citadel so that, in time of war, all his serfs could come inside the walls with their livestock. Too many people had come to depend on him. Always on the brink of financial ruin, he turned to raiding other city-states. Now people in neighboring countries called him Theseus the Pirate. But here in Athens he was still revered as a wise and just king.

He had been both these things to me. He could have locked me in a cell until the ransom was paid, with rats for company, instead of ordering pastries and making me laugh. And he was right about my fingernails, about everything. We mortals live under the rule of the gods. All we can do with destiny is learn to accept it. My destiny was to marry and to keep my husband happy.

I made up my mind to find Theseus and apologize the next morning. But I never had the chance.

CHAPTER FIVE

~⌒~

At sunrise the next morning, the first day of the third month of my kidnapping, my brothers arrived with a hundred talents of gold. There wasn't even time alone with Theseus for a proper good-bye. Castor and Polydeuces were hungry for a fight. The ransom had been a great sacrifice for Sparta and, as always, my brothers' heavenly honor was at stake. But they were guests in the Athens citadel; it would have been a breach of hospitality to throw the first punch. Polydeuces, a champion boxer, worked hard to provoke Theseus into hitting him first.

Theseus gave no such excuse, ignoring their taunts about the cowardice of piracy compared to a good, clean battle to win spoils. Instead, he played the perfect host with a mocking smile that made both brothers white-lipped with fury by the time my new wardrobe was packed.

"Chin up, you'll do fine," Theseus called to me as I waited for the horses to be hitched to the chariot.

I turned and waved my hand.

"Such a fine gentleman . . ." Hessia, standing behind me, sobbed against my shoulder.

When I got home to Sparta, my foal Thunder was a hand taller and frolicking with his mother. I would have liked to begin training him with the bit, but they didn't want me down in the paddock. It was unladylike and, besides, I would get dirty. The serious business of becoming the bride of a king had begun, whether I was ready for it or not.

Two suitors were already waiting at the palace, Ajax of Salamis and Palamedes of Euboea. Ajax was the largest man I had ever seen; I was terrified of him. Palamedes was lean and sharp, like a hunting dog, with shrewd gray eyes. The next to arrive was also named Ajax. This one, son of King Oileus of Locris, was a head shorter than Ajax of Salamis and of much smaller build. He was rumored to be the swiftest runner in all the Greek lands. It was amusing to see them together, the great, hulking warrior and the tightly built athlete. My brothers began calling them Greater and Lesser Ajax. The names stuck, and the two became inseparable companions.

The rest of the kings were on their way. Word of my kidnapping had spread throughout Greece, and each one wanted to stake his claim before I was abducted by one of the others.

"You've become an obsession," Theseus had warned. "Your father will have to find some way of choosing one of them without becoming a sworn enemy of all the others. His troubles are just beginning."

In this prediction Theseus had been correct. By the month of the grape harvest eleven of Greece's most powerful warriors had assembled in Sparta, all promising magnificent marriage gifts. Cinyras of Cyprus, already married to the daughter of a vanquished neighbor, was promising to dispose of his wife.

My father, Tyndareus, who preferred hunting and horse racing to diplomacy, walked around muttering to himself. He made no promises, because he was too afraid of promoting a war inside our citadel, with all the losers united against the winner and against Sparta. As winter rains descended, the suitors grew more and more restless. To distract them, Father staged daily hunts and nightly banquets. This hospitality, so soon after the ransom to Theseus, was a drain on the royal treasury.

Hessia presided over servant gossip in the courtyard, where her stories of fabulous Athens soon became tiresome. The kitchen slaves told her they wanted to hear no more about the delicate almond pastries served by Theseus every afternoon. More and more, talk centered on what the suitors were saying about one another behind closed doors, on which king or prince would arrive next. One day I caught them placing bets on who would win me. I wanted to shout that I was a person, not a prize stag in a hunting competition. But they would only have laughed at such a comparison, and Hessia would have told me to stop putting on airs.

Hessia put her coins on Menelaus, younger brother of Agamemnon, who was high king over all Greece. In a way Menelaus and I were already related. My elder sister, Clytemnestra, was married to the great Agamemnon. Clytemnestra sent a private messenger announcing her brother-in-law's arrival, urging me to look with favor upon him and describing the riches that would be mine as his wife.

"Menelaus talks of nothing but Helen of the Flaxen Hair," my sister's runner whispered in my ear. "You seem to have the power to make men your slaves. Be sure you use it to buy the best possible position for yourself and your children. A word from you might sway Father's decision, so remember this: Menelaus may not look like much, but even as junior princess of Mycenae, you'll have all of Greece at your feet."

This power fascinated me. All the warriors camped in our great hall could have snapped me like a sapling in their bare hands, yet several blushed and stammered in my presence, especially the great, lumbering Ajax.

Why shouldn't I use this power Clytemnestra described instead of sneaking around the palace like a frightened mouse, trying to keep out of their way? And why shouldn't *I* have a say in this decision? After all, *I* was the one who would spend the rest of my life with one of these strangers, giving birth to his children, sharing his table and his bed.

When I was summoned to meet Menelaus, I rubbed kohl around my eyes and put on a pale blue robe embroidered with silver flowers. My mirror was indeed inferior to those in Athens. But even in its bumpy surface, the princess in the mirror was still there, looking back at me. I draped a shimmering silver veil over my head and looked again. She was beautiful. *I* was beautiful.

I set out for the men's quarters, determined to be more like my sister, Clytemnestra.

CHAPTER SIX

❧

"S he glows, like a beacon in a stormy night," Menelaus was saying to Father. "I haven't seen her since my brother's wedding. She was still a child. I'm quite ... overcome."

One of our maids was washing the road dust from his feet. He pushed her aside and strode toward me, then stopped short as if unsure of what to do next.

I imagined myself as his wife, decked in gold and precious jewels, and having to submit to his embraces whenever he wanted me. I imagined myself locked in his hairy, sinewy arms. "Welcome to Sparta, Prince Menelaus. You honor our kingdom," I said, forcing a smile. I couldn't wait to get back to the women's quarters to describe him to Penelope: the squat torso, the square-cut red hair, the down-slanted eyes that would hold no humor.

He drew in his breath as if surprised I possessed the gift of speech. His eyes never left me as he addressed my father. "Her hair . . . spun gold. Skin like warm honey. Eyes the color of the Aegean at dusk. She's as beautiful as Aphrodite." He shook himself then and pulled away his gaze. "I'm usually a plain man, not given to foolish poetry."

My father was enjoying our highborn guest's confusion. "Don't apologize," he said. "Helen's beauty leaves poets dumb, makes quiet men eloquent."

Theseus wanted me to feel proud of my divine beauty. My sister, Clytemnestra, wanted me to make the most of the power it gave me. But hearing myself praised like this always made me feel guilty of some unnamed sin. There were too many stories of the gods' vengeance whenever any mortal mimicked their perfection. Aphrodite, Goddess of Love and Beauty, was especially fond of changing her competition into toads and lizards.

As soon as Father dismissed me, I ran to find my cousin. Penelope was waiting for me on a bench under our favorite olive tree. "Well?" she asked, setting down her embroidery.

"He looks like an arrogant bulldog. Didn't once speak to me, just described me out loud to Father. Same old comparisons. The spun-gold hair, eyes the color of the Aegean."

"Don't be so hard on the man; he probably thought it improper to speak directly to you, an untouched maid. And you really are quite . . . spectacular." She reached to readjust my heavy braid. She had plaited it earlier this morning, interweaving strands of hair with a garland of flowers, one of the new Athenian hairstyles we were trying to imitate. "Poor man, he's obviously smitten, like all the others—sit still while I tuck in the ends—How many have been just passing through our remote mountain kingdom since you returned?"

"Eleven—no, twelve, counting Menelaus."

"Has he made an offer?"

"I don't want to marry him; he has hairy arms."

I stole a glance at Penelope, wondering for the thousandth time how she felt about my extraordinary success in the marriage market she herself seemed so eager to enter. Penelope was as dark as I was blond, the classic Greek princess. Of the two of us, she was the prize, if any of the suitors had the wit to know it. She always knew what to do, no matter what the predicament, and she excelled in the household arts. She could weave hunts and battles into tapestries that were a joy to see. She wove stories, too, to fill long winter evenings. Even the court bard would sit and listen to her. She made me feel safe.

"Let's run away to the mountains, just the two of us," I said, seizing her hands. "We can live on nuts and figs and not marry anyone."

"We'd starve to death in the mountains," she said, laughing, "or be captured by bandits! In the end your father will have to choose one of them—and I will marry one of the leftovers," she added after a pause. She sat staring at the grove of olive trees, their silvery leaves suddenly still. Dark clouds had gathered, and the smell of an impending storm mingled with the odor of wild oregano.

"Why must that *be*?" I insisted. "Why must we wait to be chosen—like melons? They go on about my hair and eyes. None of them care about the person inside!"

She smiled and shook her head. "Even if you must wait to be chosen, you are nothing like a melon. And your husband will learn to love the person inside, who is no less beautiful." She brushed a wisp of hair from my forehead. "Fair Helen of the Flaxen Hair, isn't it also exciting to be you? *Isn't* it? You like the pretty clothes, the new hairdos, don't you?"

Sometimes it *was* exciting, sitting with Penelope making fun of the suitors: Cinyras, who cheated shamelessly at draughts, a betting game played on small tables in the men's hall, and poor, lumbering Ajax, who no longer frightened me. But sometimes I fantasized about running away to Theseus in Athens. And sometimes my anger astonished me, erupting over the most trivial things. Most of the time during those months I didn't know what I was feeling.

The suitors hunted and gambled and emptied more and more amphorae of wine. They pressured my father for a decision and gave one another glowering looks that led to frequent fights. Even the two Ajaxes came to blows after one week of nonstop rain. No one knew where it would end.

And then Odysseus came. He was king of a small island named Ithaca. Hessia said he was a fool to think he might be in the running. Unlike the others, he owned no gold-trimmed armor, no silver serving dishes. His rocky terrain wasn't even suited for horses.

"He's always had a nerve, that one," said Hessia.

For once I agreed with her. Odysseus had visited our court a year earlier. I remembered him always off in some corner thinking his own thoughts. When he did speak, it was a clever pun or a probing question that left me tongue-tied. I was glad he was too poor to be a serious candidate.

Penelope defended him. "He has as much to offer as any man here—and more brains than all the others combined. . . ." She caught herself then and gave me the strangest look.

Soon after the arrival of the tall, sandy-haired Ithacan in his simple, undyed tunic and leather vest, Penelope became moody and pensive, not at all like herself. Several times I caught her talking quietly with him in the king's private garden. Once I heard the peal of her laughter and wondered what she could find amusing about anything Odysseus would have to say. It was forbidden for an unmarried woman to be alone with a man, and I marveled at her boldness. Still, for all our closeness, I was afraid to ask her about these meetings.

"You look different," I said one evening as she stepped out of the bath.

She blushed and pulled a towel around her, although there was no need for modesty with only a slave girl and me in the room.

"How could I be different?" she asked, not meeting my eyes.

"I don't know, glowing, beautiful. . . ."

"Don't talk nonsense, Helen. You're the beauty here."

But she was lying. Standing there in her white towel, flushed from the hot water, Penelope had been feeling like the most beautiful woman on earth.

CHAPTER SEVEN

❧

I heard about Odysseus's solution to the problem of the suitors from the servants. "Who would have thought of it? It's the only way to prevent bloodshed," Hessia was saying to her cronies, who had gathered at the well in the central courtyard to draw water and begin the daylong exchange of gossip. I hid behind a pillar and waited for her to go on. Hessia paused for effect, like the storytellers in the market do, and her listeners set down their jugs and waited to hear the rest. The women of the household had already taken their morning baths, lunch was hours away, the sun was warm, and there is nothing the Greeks love more than a good talk.

"I always knew young Odysseus had a head on those broad shoulders," Hessia finally said, revising her former opinion of the Ithacan king. "We'll have a decision before tomorrow. Mark my words."

I didn't stay to hear the rest. The idea, whatever it was, had something to do with choosing a husband for me. I crossed the courtyard at a run, scattering some geese that were pecking wheat from a trough.

My father was up in the gallery above the men's hall, shouting to gain the attention of the suitors, who were down below in the vestibule, reclining on couches around the central hearth, drinking wine and playing draughts.

"I have news you are all eager to hear," Tyndareus yelled above the boom of male laughter. My brother Castor stood glowering at a particularly rowdy table of players—both Greater and Lesser Ajaxes and Idomeneus of Crete. Ignoring my father's pleas for silence, these three had continued calling out their bets.

Father saw me then and beckoned for me to join him. I adjusted my veil to cover my hair. Eyes downcast, I crossed the hall, edging past spears and shields and hunting dogs sprawled at their masters' feet. As I climbed the stairs to stand by his side, the noise diminished.

"Whoever wants to be considered for Helen's hand will have to swear a sacred oath," Father shouted into the sudden hush.

The suitors all wanted to be considered, interrupting with shouts of assent while devouring me with their eyes. Greater Ajax banged the butt of his shield against the floor for emphasis.

I looked down, wondering which one I would prefer if the choice were mine. I had no real feelings about any of them, except that some frightened me more than others.

"Hear me out!" Father was saying. "You'll first have to swear that whomever I choose as my daughter's husband, the rest of you will defend him from any man who envies his good fortune and tries to steal her away. *For the rest of your lives!*"

The shouts subsided.

"As if he were your blood brother. . . ."

The suitors eyed one another uncomfortably as the implications of this promise became clear. If a man swore this oath and then wasn't chosen, not only was he prevented from making war on my husband, he was also honor-bound to protect the man. The logic was simple—and brilliant. There would be no warfare among the suitors.

My father signaled ushers to refill the wine cups. "We will pour our libations to Thundering Zeus and drink to this agreement," he announced.

Later they sacrificed a horse at the altar underneath the gallery. It went forward to its death without a struggle, a good omen, showing the oath favorable to the gods and making it doubly binding. The priests cut the carcass into twelve sections. That night each suitor would stand next to one of them and repeat the oath. They planned to bury all twelve pieces in a mound that would be called the Horse's Tomb.

"There are only twelve portions and thirteen suitors," I pointed out to my father after the sacrifice.

"Odysseus was never in competition," he said. "I've awarded him Penelope in exchange for his solution. To judge from the whispering in corners that's been going on, I suspect she'll make no protest."

I didn't catch the rest of his words. All I could think of was that Penelope would go away to Ithaca, a rocky island many days' voyage across dangerous, unpredictable seas. How blind I'd been! They'd been falling in love right in front of my eyes, and I'd never seen it! I was halfway up the stairs to the women's quarters when the anger hit.

She hadn't said a word! We'd shared secrets all our lives and she hadn't said a word!

"This was *her* doing, this Oath of the Horse," I snapped at Hessia, who was unfolding a skein of aqua wool from one of the wicker boxes where such supplies were kept. "Why didn't she *tell* me?" I kicked at my cousin's loom and sent it crashing to the floor.

Hessia clucked her tongue at the sprawl of wood and wool. "What does it matter whose solution it was? It's what we needed to get you married off. . . ."

"I don't *want* to be married off," I sobbed. "I just want us to stay the way we were."

"She doesn't belong to you," Hessia said, shaking her head, and then, after a silence, "She's given her heart to him. She belongs to him now. You'll feel that way about your husband." She reached to wipe my tears.

"No, I won't. Not ever."

Biting my lip, I knelt to pick up the loom.

P enelope found me under our olive tree, where I sat playing a sad Athenian tune on my flute. "I didn't mean to exclude you," she began. "But until Odysseus proposed the idea, man to man, I wanted no rumors to turn your father against it."

That was not likely, I thought, but I said nothing. She was so afraid of ruining her fragile happiness.

"Will you give us your blessing?" she asked, taking my hand awkwardly.

I hugged her close. The grief of losing her had become a dull pain inside my rib cage. "I'm sorry about the loom," I whispered.

"Odysseus fixed it, better than new. He's wonderful with his hands. He's going to make me a larger one when we get home to Ithaca. . . ."

Home to Ithaca! I made an excuse about some errand that needed my attention and left Penelope with Hessia, who had been watching us from the shade of the citadel walls. Penelope was describing the palace in Ithaca. By all accounts, it was no more than a country manor. It could have been a shack and she would have found something to praise.

My father's long-awaited announcement came the following morning, a kind of anticlimax. Hessia won the bet in the servants' quarters. Menelaus of Mycenae would be my husband.

"You will be daughter to the great house of Mycenae," my father told me. "Their wealth is legendary."

An expression of gratitude was expected. "You honor me, Father," I said in a small voice, looking down at my feet. In a world we do not control, acceptance is the only response. I told myself that Menelaus would be no worse than any of the others and better than some, that I would get used to him.

My fiancé presented his betrothal gifts in my father's private garden, gold rings and necklaces, a set of bronze serving bowls, a silver flute with perfect pitch.

I was touched that Menelaus had bothered to find out I played the flute. The stocky warrior was almost too moved for speech. "You can play for me when we're married," he stammered, blushing to the roots of his red hair. He grasped my hand. "Helen, the gods have made me the happiest of men!"

"The honor is mine, Lord Menelaus," I said, and pulled my hand from his iron grip.

He had also brought a gold diadem. I'd never seen such a lavish piece. I remember thinking that Mycenae must be wealthy beyond belief if women wore such headpieces. Its chains of gold coins would have reached well below my shoulders. But before Menelaus could place it on my head, he dropped it on the floor.

Helping to pick it up, I heard myself saying all the right things. "Thank you, my lord. I will straighten the strands back in the women's quarters."

It occurred to me then that Theseus would be pleased. I was behaving like the perfect golden princess.

Penelope was a radiant bride, and Odysseus's joy softened his features, so that I found him handsome for the first time. I tried not to begrudge them their happiness. All my life I had been half in awe and half jealous of Penelope's intelligence, her ability to put people at ease and make things right. Now she had managed to outshine me in what should have been my moment of glory. After all, I caught myself thinking, *I* was marrying into Greece's ruling house, while she had accepted a minor chieftain.

No, that wasn't fair, I told myself firmly. The gods would surely punish such arrogance. Penelope's marriage was a simple affair compared to mine, which would be celebrated only after months of preparation. Besides, it wasn't the attention I envied. It was the look in her eyes when Odysseus took her hand to lead her away at the end of the ceremony.

That night I prayed to Aphrodite, Goddess of Love, that I

might feel this way about Menelaus. I offered libations of wine and released two white doves, the way the virgins worship her in Athens. But I mustn't have accomplished the ritual correctly, because Aphrodite didn't answer my prayers. Each time I looked at my fiancé, I felt only a stirring of pity mixed with guilt.

After the week of feasting that followed the marriage ceremony, we followed the bride and groom to the citadel gates, throwing flowers and singing hymns of praise. Odysseus and Penelope mounted their horses, a matched pair of grays that had been wedding gifts from my father. Penelope waved at me gaily, then turned her mount to follow her husband.

I sat under our tree watching until I could no longer see them on the winding trail to the sea. It didn't seem possible that I could go on living without her. It didn't seem possible that she could ride away from me without a second look.

I will never forgive her, I thought, and was at once ashamed of myself.

CHAPTER EIGHT

❧

B y the time my own marriage was celebrated, almost
a year later, both my brothers had died in a brawl
at a hunting party. Castor had picked a fight over a
matter of honor and was felled by an arrow. Polydeuces
died avenging him. The servants whispered that Zeus
received them on Mount Olympus, that they were allowed
to live on alternate days, one walking among the immortals,
the other in the grave, though how anyone could have
known such a thing was a mystery to me.

When Menelaus returned to claim me, he found himself
doubly blessed. Not only was he marrying the world's most
beautiful woman, he was inheriting a kingdom as well.
My father had lost all interest in kingship after the death
of his sons. He wanted to retire to his hunting lodge.
After our marriage Menelaus and I would rule Sparta in his
stead.

Wedding gifts poured into the main hall from all over the
civilized world. Even the disappointed suitors sent gold
wine cups and bronze cauldrons. Theseus sent a magnificent white mare, bred of Arabian stock by the Trojans in

Asia Minor, and a circular mirror of burnished bronze with a handle in the shape of the goddess Aphrodite.

Menelaus brought a second gold diadem, this one even more ornate than the betrothal crown, and managed to put it on my head without tangling the long chains that hung down alongside my face. "I want you to wear it at our wedding," he said. "It's an heirloom from the ruling house of Atreus. There are sixteen thousand gold pieces."

I tried a few tentative steps. "I'll fall over in the middle of the ceremony," I said, laughing.

"No, Helen," he said without a stammer, "I will be holding you so tightly you will not fall."

He didn't seem quite so ungainly. I wondered if I'd finally adjusted to the marriage, or if Aphrodite's blessing might be having some belated effect.

And then Penelope and Odysseus arrived. It was the first visit since their wedding. They brought fleece for our marriage bed and a linen cover into which Penelope had woven the story of the twelve suitors swearing the Oath of the Horse. On the border a red-haired Menelaus was stepping forward to claim me, a tiny figure wearing a gold diadem that threatened to topple her.

My cousin had much to tell me about Ithaca's slower island rhythms, about Odysseus's old nurse, Euryleia, who was even bossier than Hessia, about the improvements they'd made to the palace.

"Odysseus made our bed out of olive wood," she told me. "There's not another like it in all the world!"

"Come now, Penelope, you're exaggerating. A bed is a bed."

"This one is unique—Oh, I'll tell you the secret, only

you—Odysseus carved it out of a huge olive tree that's *still rooted* in the earth. He's built our new bedroom around it! Everyone knows olive trees live forever. Odysseus says the magic forces of the tree pulse through us as we lie there. We're sure to produce strong sons and faithful daughters. . . ."

She blushed then and I changed the subject. I didn't want to hear about magic beds. I didn't want to think about Penelope and Odysseus locked in each other's arms. Even if I was finding Menelaus less offensive, I realized listening to her that I was never going to feel that kind of passion for him. But Penelope was bursting with pride, and I was her oldest confidante. She couldn't have known how painful her stories were for me.

The day before the wedding, as was our custom, I offered my playthings to Artemis—a terra-cotta rabbit, an old ceramic doll, even my favorite set of knucklebones, inlaid with silver and brass, although many grown women continued to play this game. I baked a loaf of bread, which I offered with prayers to Demeter, the goddess of the harvest. Finally, I filled a basket with sacred barley groats and sacrificed to Aphrodite. This time I didn't ask for so much. "Help me to be a good wife and mother," I prayed, arms raised palms upward, facing her altar. "And a good queen to my people."

My father sacrificed one hundred oxen in honor of our union. He could afford to be generous. Menelaus's bride-price would enrich Sparta with two hundred oxen, two hundred sheep, one thousand goats, and four matched chariot horses. Many of these animals would be delivered the following spring, but the ones he brought with him filled the corrals outside the citadel and the commons inside the walls, so that it was almost impossible to walk through these areas.

The gallery that adjoined the main courtyard was just as impassable, with oxen to be slaughtered, their necks draped with garlands of flowers, horses tethered to columns, slaves rolling jugs of wine or scurrying toward the women's quarters, their arms piled high with holiday clothing from the storerooms.

I had invited Theseus in spite of my father's protests. My brothers could no longer start a fight, and Menelaus wanted me to include anyone I wished. He promised to deal courteously with my former kidnapper.

Arms crossed and eyes twinkling, the old Athenian stood watching as Menelaus led me away at the end of the marriage ritual. I had practiced walking with the Mycenaean diadem on my head, and I did not once falter. I felt completely grown-up that morning, as if I had stepped through a door into a new, adult world.

Later, at the wedding feast, I caught Theseus looking at me and held up my hand to display long, painted nails. The old pirate nodded and winked.

"Are you still seeking the mystery of love?" he asked when we had a moment to talk privately.

"I've given up on love," I said.

"Good. Let's hope it never finds you."

"How can you say that, after all you shared with Hippolyta?"

"What we shared was a mixed blessing, with equal parts pain. Listen, girl, Menelaus will be an impeccable husband. He's a good man, if somewhat lacking in imagination, and he loves you more than he should." Theseus reached for my hands. "Here is the last piece of advice I'll ever give you: Be satisfied with what you've got."

CHAPTER NINE

❦

The first five years of marriage I worked at following Theseus's advice. Menelaus was a good king and a good husband. I grew fond of him. Even the duties of the marriage bed were less awful than I had imagined. On the eve of my wedding Hessia had given her final lecture on the subject of sex. "Just close your eyes and think of something pleasant," she said, patting my hand. "It will all be over in a few minutes." After a while I was able to look back on that and laugh.

I tried not to think about Penelope and Odysseus in their olive tree bed. I remembered to count my blessings; there was much to be thankful for. The gods were good to us, our harvests bountiful, our state prosperous and peaceful. I had my daily routine, servants to supervise, quarrels to mediate, wool and flax to dye and weave into fine cloth I was proud of.

Our daughter, Hermione, was born one year after our wedding, on the first day of the month of wine-making, an easy labor, unusual with the first child. She was pinkcheeked and strawberry blond, with my smile and Menelaus's quiet disposition.

• • •

M y husband did not scold me for failing to produce a son. He stayed for hours beside her crib, making up silly songs and letting her grip his thick, calloused fingers in her tiny hands. As she grew, he carved wooden dolls and miniature animals for her. When she turned two, he taught her to ride a pony he had trained especially.

Our men ride beardless and short-haired into battle, so that the enemy cannot grab them by the hair. Menelaus let his beard grow, a sign to all the world that he had finished with warfare. His warriors joked about their king's preference for riding in the paddock with the castle children instead of leading raiding parties to neighboring city-states.

I can't isolate the moment when the mood of the nation began to shift, but there was a subtle change in the air before our daughter's fourth birthday. Talk of war had begun to spread in the marketplace and in the servants' quarters. Apparently, these rumors had reached the islands even before they reached us. Penelope's son, born a year earlier, was named Telemachus, which means "final battle." This choice of name had to do with a great war the oracles had been predicting for years, to be waged between Greece and Troy, a wealthy civilization across the Aegean Sea.

When Penelope visited just before Hermione's birthday, she could talk of nothing but her fears for Odysseus. According to an oracle who read the flights of birds, her husband would leave home to fight on foreign soil and not return for twenty years, reaching Ithaca ragged and unrecognized. Odysseus had originally planned to come to Sparta with his wife and son, but he had stayed behind to strengthen the fortifications of the home castle.

Penelope's visit should have been a happy time for us, watching our children romp together in the wild anemones that carpeted the hills, talking and laughing over our memories. but she was sunk so deeply into gloom, it was impossible to console her. And Telemachus, though a well-formed, healthy boy, seemed to pick up on her mood. He cried each time his mother left his sight. At the end of the month I was relieved to see them go.

"Do *you* think Greece will go to war against the Trojans?" I asked my husband.

"If we can find a good enough excuse. Troy is the wealthiest city on earth. Their king, Priam, controls the Hellespont—a narrow entrance to the Black Sea—and collects duty on all the goods that come in and out. The Trojans are admirable people, and Priam never fails to honor his gods. But my brother, Agamemnon, is tired of paying double for hides and spice and for the corn we depend on from Asia Minor. Knowing Agamemnon, he's also itching to feel the heft of a good sword in his hand."

"Would we go to war over customs duty?" I asked.

"We'd have to do better than that. The gods would never favor such a self-serving excuse." My husband noticed my expression then and hurried to reassure me. "Don't worry, my dear. *I* have no wish to battle Trojans. The gods have granted me a simpler destiny." Hermione was at his feet trying to scoop up knucklebones in one small fist. He picked her up and bounced her on his knee. "I have everything a man could wish for right here."

But Penelope's moods had always been contagious. I continued to brood. I knew nothing of war, but I knew what it felt like to be kidnapped by enemy warriors. I knew what happened to women and children when their men were not home to protect them. Against my will I was drawn to each new rumor in the servants' quarters.

Menelaus laughed at my fears. Still, he must have seen some need for diplomacy between our two nations, because he himself opened negotiations with the Trojans for better trade concessions, taking advantage of an earlier acquaintance with Troy's royal family.

But the gods do not always support our noble intentions, and it was, in the end, these negotiations that sealed our fate, once and for all. Because before the next harvest Greece got its excuse for a war against Troy, and Menelaus could do nothing to avoid being drawn into it.

CHAPTER TEN

❦

The fates ought to have given warning that my small, safe world was about to shift on its axis, but I received none. In fact, I had begun to feel more optimistic about the future. As a result of my husband's gifts and messages, we were expecting a diplomatic mission from Troy. A prominent Trojan prince was arriving to talk about trade and tariffs. According to Menelaus, it was perhaps also a gesture on Troy's part to squelch rumors of this impending war the oracles seemed to enjoy promoting.

"On my last visit to Troy," my husband told me, "I struck up a friendship with the second of Priam's fifty sons, a young man named Paris Alexandros. I told him he should come to Greece, see the lands and islands beyond Troy's lofty walls. He's finally acting on that invitation. The lad spent his early years as a shepherd, before being reunited with his royal family. But I'll let *him* tell you the story. Paris is a born storyteller."

We had ordered a banquet in the Trojan's honor, and the palace hummed with preparations. As an added honor we went down to the harbor to meet his ship ourselves.

I rode my white mare down the rocky trail. It felt wonderful to be on horseback under the bright autumn sky, my fears so suddenly put to rest. I found myself thinking of an earlier trip down to the sea, on the bay mare Theseus had stolen for me. I remembered the late summer heat, the taste of dust and fear.

When we reached the water, the Trojan's galley had already rounded the point. Our slaves set up a sunshade on the beach. For the next hour we watched it approach, its square sail bobbing above a shimmering sea. Hermione scurried about collecting shells and asking questions about boats and fishes.

I watched her, still remembering that sea voyage six years earlier. It seemed another lifetime. Where had that frightened girl gone? Did she live somewhere inside the contented wife and mother, the calm-eyed queen who sponsored festivals and led the temple dances? It occurred to me then, sitting there beside my husband, watching the Trojan ship draw closer, that the gods hadn't given me such a bad destiny after all.

I saw a fair-haired figure come forward on the deck. Menelaus stood to shout a welcome. The vermillion galley glided closer. The sun gleamed on the Trojan's golden hair. He was poised in the prow, his hair curled against his magnificent head, his body bronzed and muscular, like a statue of a prizewinning athlete. Although he stood perfectly still, bracing himself against the mast, I knew he would be graceful in motion, like a mountain cat.

"Is that Apollo, who drives the sun chariot?" asked Hermione in a loud whisper, and everyone laughed.

"He's a man, not a god," Menelaus explained. "But Apollo must have touched him with beauty. His name is Paris, and he comes to us from across the sea."

I lost my heart to him before the hull grated against the sand. All at once I understood how Penelope could have left me to follow Odysseus anywhere on earth, and I forgave her for it.

Hessia would say I was bewitched by Aphrodite, struck by one of her invisible love arrows. If this sudden passion was Aphrodite's doing, I forgave her too.

He leaped from the ship and bounded up the beach to embrace Menelaus at the water's edge. Afterward he walked toward me, smiling a secret smile as if conscious of his heart-stopping grace. It was a joy to watch him move.

I don't remember if I managed to say anything. He took my hand, his fingers warm, his eyes a blazing blue. "Helen, your beauty is for immortals to describe. For once in my life I'm speechless."

"Are you all right, my dear?" Menelaus asked me later at the banquet.

I wasn't all right. I felt sure everyone in the hall was watching me gaze with desire at the golden Trojan prince. I mumbled something about the heat of the journey. "I'm not feeling well; I should go back to my rooms."

"But Paris is getting ready to tell his story."

"If you leave now," said our guest, looking straight into my soul, "I will consider it an unforgivable breach of etiquette."

Almighty Zeus, he knows! I thought. He's probably used to watching his comrades' wives fall in love with him.

Paris stood and downed his wine. "It's my turn to tell of my misdeeds," he announced to the upturned faces.

I leaned forward, clenching my hands in my lap as he began to speak.

"When my mother, Queen Hecuba of Troy, was pregnant with me, she dreamed of giving birth to a bundle of burning sticks. Of course, an oracle pronounced this a bad omen and advised the king to get rid of me as soon as I was born. So there I was, barely out of the womb, and a death sentence on my head!" Paris paused to drink, drawing out the suspense. "As is customary in such cases, my father asked a servant to take me to the mountainside and leave me for wolves to devour." He laughed at our shocked expressions. "Don't despair, dear audience. Oracles, who must always be coming up with new predictions to earn their keep, sometimes lie. As you see, I am here fully developed, and Troy grown prosperous beyond belief. Now, where did I leave off? The servant, a simple shepherd, didn't have the heart to leave me there. . . ."

I didn't catch all the words. I was lost in the sound of his voice, mesmerized as he licked his lips, brushed a hand through his springy curls. Besides, I had already heard the story from Hessia, who had it from the Trojan servants.

The shepherd had raised Paris as his own son. Fifteen years after his rescue, and still ignorant of his true identity, Paris showed up for the annual games at the great citadel of Troy. He entered the running event and outran all forty-nine Trojan princes, his full and half brothers. Then he beat them at archery and spear throwing.

The third eldest of Priam's sons, named Deiphobus, wanted to kill the upstart peasant who had dared beat them at their own games. But the elderly shepherd rushed forward and announced that they would be killing their own brother. I couldn't remember all the details, but somehow King Priam and Queen Hecuba welcomed their lost son with great rejoicing.

"The oracles are still mumbling about me," Paris concluded, flashing his smile. "But my father is no longer listening. Besides, they'll change their tune when I return to Troy with the greatest treasure our fabled city has ever known." He looked at me across the table, and the rest of the world ceased to exist.

CHAPTER ELEVEN

For three days I watched the main courtyard from my window, my heart thudding each time he appeared. Hessia watched me, shaking her head. Then Menelaus insisted on my appearance at a feast to celebrate a successful hunt. "You've been keeping too much to the women's quarters," he said, "and I enjoy showing you off."

I changed robes six times, discarding them in a heap on the floor, wishing I knew what women were wearing in fabulous Troy. I finally sent Hessia to the storeroom to find the sea green robe I had worn that first day in Athens, years before. It still fit, but it was shorter, exposing more of my calves.

Hessia clucked her tongue.

"Everyone knows Spartan women wear the shorter chiton," I protested.

"Not married women. It's indecent."

I looked at myself in the looking glass that had been Theseus's wedding present, remembering the princess in the mirror. "I like it," I said, and left the room before she could scold me further.

The men had finished dessert and begun the drinking. They were throwing dice and betting heavily, downing their fifth or sixth cups by the time I arrived. Fists pounded tables; male laughter echoed from the ceiling. Ushers were mixing wine in bronze cauldrons; slaves scurried about delivering it to Trojan guests and to our own noblemen.

"Helen!" Menelaus called out. "Come sit across from me so that I might feast my eyes on the fairest sight in all of Greece!" His speech was slurred, his eyes unfocused.

I was searching the room for Paris when he came and sat beside me on the bench facing Menelaus's couch. He offered me wine, which I declined. I didn't trust my hands to pick up the cup.

"Ah, this is better courtesy to a guest," said Menelaus, seeing us together. "Get her to play for you," he told Paris. "Helen's music would tame wild beasts."

"Would you like me to get my flute?" I asked, looking down at my hands.

"Stay. You entertain me just sitting here."

At first I could find nothing to say. He talked easily about Troy and his family and told a funny story about learning how to ride wild ponies in the mountains. After a while I heard myself telling him about my kidnapping and my unexpected friendship with Theseus.

Menelaus was concentrating on a betting game called Game of Cities, played with five small stones on a board divided into five sections. He paid no attention to our conversation. The hall couldn't have been noisier, but I only remember the quiet, the sense of isolation that separated us from the others. So that I could hear him above the din,

Paris had to lean toward me and speak his words into my ear, his lips occasionally brushing my hair.

Finally, my husband slumped backward on the couch; his silver wine cup clattered to the floor. Blush red wine spilled onto the marble.

"The king has earned the right to a short respite," Paris shouted above the men's catcalls. "If it hadn't been for his well-aimed arrows to that charging boar, some of us would be on our funeral pyres instead of drinking and carousing here. Let us fill our cups and pour our drops to Apollo, who guides the arrows of the faithful."

His toast produced a chorus of cheers and another drunken replay of the hunt. Their attention was diverted from us.

We talked no more. I studied the shadow of his thick lashes and the smooth line of his jaw, which I longed to trace with my fingers. Then he kneeled forward to pick up Menelaus's cup. He stayed there, trailing his finger in the spilled wine on the floor. I realized that he was forming letters. I watched as each took shape and then faded almost as quickly as it had appeared. I . . . love . . . Helen. His message complete, Paris turned and looked up at me, smiling.

"Do you think your diplomatic status would protect you if my husband awoke and caught you writing . . . such nonsense? What if the servants had seen?"

"Better to die for those words than to leave them unsaid!" He seized my hand. "Where can we be alone?"

"We *can't* be alone."

"Then I'll have to kiss you right here."

"You're insane."

"*Yes!*"

We were both insane. We arranged, in whispers, to leave the hall separately and meet in the lemon grove. Paris left first. I stayed behind, willing myself to appear normal, listening to my heart pound. I trembled at each clash of wine cups, each burst of laughter, praying it would not wake my husband. I studied the faces of his warriors. Had any of them noticed or were they too drunk to notice anything?

At last I stood up. Still sprawled on his couch, Menelaus shifted position. I stopped breathing until his snoring resumed. Then I walked toward the doorway on legs that didn't feel like my own.

He was waiting for me, his fair hair glowing in the moonlight. My fears evaporated, and I ran toward him, heedless of whoever might have been outside watching. We fell into each other's arms and declared our love in the same breath.

"You were not surprised by my declaration?" I asked, moments later, holding his face between my hands. "Do women just naturally fall in love with you wherever you go?"

"Not quite everywhere. There was one on Rhodes, I believe, who did not." He laughed, capturing my hands and covering them with kisses. "But I knew *you* loved me that first moment on the beach. Because Aphrodite herself promised you to me."

"Why should she do that?"

"You were a bribe, in a beauty contest. Almost two years ago. I was summoned, by order of Zeus, to be the judge. Three goddesses—Hera, Athena, and Aphrodite—were fighting over a golden apple inscribed 'for the most beautiful.' Like peasant wives at the fish market. Someone had to settle the dispute, and this was a task Zeus didn't relish. Even the forger of thunderbolts feared the displeasure of the two losers."

"And *you* were to make that judgement?"

"Yes, love, unwillingly, but who can deny a god's summons? I'd earned a reputation during my shepherd days, judging wrestling contests and squabbles over stray sheep. Of course, I'd never reckoned on anything this grand. Each of the contestants sidled up, offering bribes. I won't bore you with the other two—invincibility in battle, emperor of Asia, that sort of thing. But Aphrodite promised the love of the most beautiful woman on earth. And everyone knows who that is. . . ."

I stood on tiptoe and lifted my chin for another of his practiced kisses, which were nothing at all like the awkward embraces of my husband.

"I gave the apple to her, of course, and here we are," he said, and then held me at arm's length, eyes glowing with appreciation.

For the first time in my life I felt truly beautiful, deep inside. Tonight as I dressed to come down to the banquet, I *was* the princess in the mirror. I finally understood the mystery of her smile.

"It's taken a year to talk my father into this 'diplomatic mission,' arrange for the ship. Immortal gods, I thought I would never feel you in my arms!" He pulled me closer and I stopped thinking, stopped worrying that we had stayed away from the great hall too long, that Menelaus might awake and ask where I was.

"How long will it take to get your things together? We can have the galley ready to sail at first light." He wasn't asking. He just assumed I would be leaving with him.

"Leave Menelaus?" I said slowly. "He'd have to be dead, not drunk. They'd catch us before we got to the coast." I shivered. *And what of Hermione? Could I commit the sin of taking her with me? Could I commit the sin of leaving her behind?*

"What's the matter, my love? You want to come with me, don't you?"

"My daughter. How can I take her on such a voyage?"

"There's ample room for her on board," he said. "Take your nurse as well, anything that makes you happy." But I knew from his eyes that he hadn't counted on the child.

"Have no fear," he said, touching my cheek. "Aphrodite has promised you to me. She'll send us a sign."

For him, it was that simple.

CHAPTER TWELVE

❧

Aphrodite's sign arrived the following morning. A messenger from Mycenae arrived with news that Menelaus's uncle had died on the island of Crete. Agamemnon wanted his brother at the funeral rites. As quickly as my husband could gather a company of warriors, he rode off through the citadel gates, leaving me to rule in his place. Unsuspecting to the end, Menelaus was pleased Paris would be staying on.

"The boy is amusing," he told me, "and not so light-willed as you might think. You can rely on him if you need a man."

I was moving in a dream, packing Hermione's things, when Hessia came upon me. She stood in the doorway, hands on hips. "So you're going off with him?"

"You can't stop me!"

"I know better than to try. It's the gods' madness. I know the signs." She came and took the pile of tunics from my arms. "You can follow your Trojan wherever you like, but Hermione stays here. Wait!" She lifted a palm to still my protest. "You've seen Menelaus with his child. What has he done that you would punish him so?"

"I can't leave her behind."

"Have you thought of what the mighty King Priam is going to think of you?"

I stood shaking my head, afraid of the answer.

"I'll tell you what he'll think: that you're his son's latest whore!"

I slapped her hard. She stepped back, rubbing her cheek. I had never hit her before; she'd been more like family than a servant.

"I love him!" I sobbed.

She shook her head pityingly, as if I had contracted a terrible disease. "Love," she sniffed, and then, "if you try to take her, I'll rouse the guards."

Still, Hessia helped me pack the gold and silver from the locked storeroom, frowning at the more valuable pieces but saying nothing.

"I refuse to go to him empty-handed, like the daughter of a poor retainer. Besides, I'm not taking anything that wasn't mine. By birthright!"

She shook her head.

"I've left everything Menelaus brought from Mycenae, the silver cups, the bronze cauldrons, all the gold."

She nodded at the gold diadem I had been wrapping in silk. It was the smaller one, which Menelaus had given me at our betrothal ceremony. He had dropped it and tangled the strands.

"This was a betrothal gift—to *me*! And I'm taking my silver flute. That was a gift too!"

Soon after sunset all the baskets were lashed to the horses and mules. But I couldn't say good-bye to my daughter. The night deepened, and I sat beside Hermione watching a smile flit across her face as she fell asleep, smoothing her red-gold curls. I wanted to offer some message of love that would make it easier for her in the morning, but there were no words to explain what I was doing. I lay beside her, drinking in the sweet smell of her skin, knowing why poets talked about hearts breaking.

"I can't *do* this!" I cried out to Hessia.

Paris, who had been pacing back and forth outside the door, came and offered me his hand. He pulled me up into his arms and kissed my tears. "Come, my love, the men are mounted and waiting. Hessia will take good care of her."

Clutching his hand, I stood in the doorway looking back at my daughter's sleeping form. I wondered if I would ever see her again in this life.

Without a word Hessia went to sit next to the bed. I saw that my nurse's hair had gone completely white—I hadn't really looked at her in years—and that she was holding her lips in a tight line to keep from crying. *I can't do this*, I thought—and followed him to the horses.

The goddess sent a full moon to speed us toward the ship. Our twisting path lay bright as day before us. I kept glancing over my shoulder, imagining shadows leaping from rocks. Menelaus's warriors had gone with him. He had left behind some elderly nobles, who could possibly have stopped us and reclaimed their lord's rightful possessions. But there was little chance of that. At dinner Paris had served some rare and delicious Rhodian wine, which he had drugged. All the men were passed out in the great hall and would sleep until noon.

Each time a loosened rock jarred the silence, Paris laughed at my startled cry. "I keep telling you, love, the gods are on our side. Don't be afraid."

In fact, our journey seemed charmed. When we reached Paris's red ship, Poseidon, God of the Sea, joined Aphrodite to bless our voyage, sending a northwest breeze rippling across the bay.

"The wind is fair," the steersman called out, and Paris threw back his head and laughed. He stood a moment on deck, watching the sails billow, his fair hair blowing around his face, his tunic fluttering across his muscled thighs. Then he turned and held out his arms to me.

At daybreak I watched the coasts of my homeland recede in a blue haze for the second time of my life, knowing that this time I was truly embarked on uncharted seas. I placed myself in the hands of the goddess Aphrodite. It was a relief to give up all pretense of control.

. "Are they expecting you to return home with me?" I asked Paris later that morning.

"You're a surprise." He laughed. "They know nothing about the 'kidnapping.'" Already the word had become our private joke.

"What will they think of me—your family?"

"They'll love you, of course. How could they not?" He bent his head to kiss the palm of my hand. "But we're in no hurry to get home."

May the gods forgive me. My memories faded. I forgot my daughter, my husband, my kingdom. As the painted ship skimmed over smooth seas, dolphins played in our wake, and we had leisure to discover each other's thoughts, each other's bodies.

Each day was a gift as precious as life itself. Most people know only one or two such days in a whole lifetime. Golden afternoons faded into blue nights. I sat on silk cushions playing my flute. Paris entertained me with songs and stories of Troy's wide avenues, its bronze statues, its high, slanted walls, impossible to scale.

I listened, smiling and nodding, drinking in his features. In truth, I had little interest in our destination. I wanted to float forever on endless gentle swells. I wanted to stop at each one of the islands, swim in the pale blue shallows, walk hand in hand in the lemon groves.

"I didn't think the gods would permit anyone to be so happy," I whispered to Paris one night as we rounded Cape Sounion. "There aren't enough sacrifices in all the world to honor Aphrodite for providing all this—and *you*!" I opened my arms to the sea, framed in dark blue mountains, the salty breeze, the one bright star overhead.

"Let's honor her, then, by enjoying each other," Paris said, and reached for me.

Across the rippled water the moon was paving a highway of spun silver. We were sailing on it straight to Troy, where Priam's sons and daughters were living their fabulous lives, unaware of our approach.

But one of them—a girl named Cassandra—knew we were on our way and trembled at the destiny we carried with us.

~ PART TWO ~

CASSANDRA'S STORY

CHAPTER ONE

The terrible visions usually came when I was awake, fluttering before my eyes like startled ghosts. This one came by night. I was dreaming about my brother Paris. He was on the ship he had painted the color of ripe pomegranates, the same ship he had sailed on the previous summer in search of adventure. I saw him beneath an awning, cross-legged on the silk cushions he imported from the Orient, handsome as ever. He wore garnet earrings in the Persian fashion. In Greece and in Troy only women wear earrings, and I remember thinking that our eldest brother, Hector, would not approve. Even as I dreamed, I wondered if some of the things Paris did were just to annoy his elder brother. Then the throbbing in my temples began, and I knew this was something more than a dream.

A second person was on board the galley, a young woman, also beautiful like my brother, also cross-legged on the silk cushions. She wore a sea green robe; a garland of flowers crowned her pale blond hair. She was playing a silver flute, and Paris was teaching her "Ena Mythos," a song he had learned as a shepherd boy in the hills above Troy.

I had always disliked this brother—his refusal to be serious about anything, his effortless charm, which made women want to throw away their virtue for one hour in his arms. Yet instead of the usual irritation, I felt a foreboding as I watched him lean forward and slip a silver bracelet in the form of a coiled snake around the woman's ankle. His hand lingered on her bare foot, then caressed her leg, the inside of her thigh.

I expected her to climb into his lap—my brother had that effect on women—but she turned and faced me, the dream spectator. Smiling the sweetest smile I had ever seen, she lifted her silver flute, holding it out as if to offer a gift.

The pain in my head was growing worse. Her flute caught the sun, and the gleam turned to fire. Flames circled her fingers and swirled up her arms as she tossed the flute out over the water. It exploded into a blazing streak and fell directly above my head.

Moaning in terror, I struggled to get out of its way. But my feet had grown roots that snaked into the rough planks of the wharf where I stood.

As I fought to wake up, I was trapped inside another dream. I was suddenly outside our city walls, surrounded by slain warriors lying naked in the mud, the armor stripped from their muscular bodies. Enough of them were still writhing against death to give the field a terrible crawling appearance. Their cries echoed off Troy's circular walls. I ran for the safety of the gates, but each footstep sank deeper into the bloodred muck.

"Zeus All Wise, *help* me! Send her *away*!" I screamed. My sister Polyxena appeared and I flailed at her with my hands.

"Cassandra, *wake up!* You're having a nightmare!"

Polyxena's face shifted into focus. I released my grip on her arms. In the light of the oil lamp I saw that the imprint of my fingers had bruised the pale skin inside her wrist. I wanted to tell her how sorry I was, but I could only sob.

Polyxena had never seen me cry before. "There now. It's all right," she said, stroking my hair. Four years younger, she was obviously enjoying the opportunity to mother me.

Then our youngest sister, Laodice, joined us on my bed. "Were you dreaming of marrying Old Coroebus? *Were* you?" Laodice asked, jumping up and down with the excitement of being roused in the middle of the night. "You were screaming and clawing the walls!"

I stopped crying and wiped my eyes. The two of them watched with badly concealed pity.

"I was *not* dreaming of marrying *Prince* Coroebus," I said to Laodice. "*And* he's only twenty-nine." I stood and adjusted my tunic, hands still shaking.

Polyxena nudged Laodice and gave a warning look.

I went to the window and looked out over Troy's great walls, glowing white in the moonlight, and the rippled plain below. "It was a bad dream . . . about a war," I said. But I knew it was no ordinary dream.

The heavenly Scorpion, greatest of constellations, stretched across the night sky. The air smelled of wild oregano. I drank in the stillness in deep breaths. The pain in my head was fading; the moonlit world was too beautiful for war. Still, I knew enough about my visions to feel fear in my throat.

"Well, I don't want you to marry him anyway," said Laodice in an effort to console me. "He never smiles."

"Why should he smile?" Polyxena interrupted. "Cassandra never even looks at him. Poor man, his heart is broken."

It was no use trying to explain my position on this marriage they were so worried about. "Polyxena," I said, "you can put your sister back to bed. Here, take your lamp, I have my own. I'm going down to the garden."

"Do you think you should go down there alone?" Polyxena asked timidly. My sisters, huddled together under the blankets, eyed me strangely. Why in the world would I want to be outside in the middle of the night?

I was used to such looks. I was, after all, the odd one in the family. Soon after my eighth birthday I began to have visions of future events, earthquakes and stillbirths, fishing boats that would never return to port. Each time these visions came true, my family seemed embarrassed, irritated, and somehow frightened of me. They refused to believe my predictions. Now, at seventeen, I had long since learned to keep them to myself.

"What will Father say if you keep chasing away suitors?" Polyxena inquired from the mound of bedclothes.

I shook my head. Discussions inside the women's quarters always came back to the same subject, the marriage market we were raised to compete in. Troy could be burning down and its women would still be talking about potential suitors.

My two sisters and I were royal children. Our father, King Priam, was renowned in all the civilized world for having sired fifty sons and almost as many daughters, though not, of course, with the same woman. Polyxena, Laodice, and I were born of the same mother, Queen Hecuba, who had distinguished herself by producing, in addition to the three of us, six surviving heirs to the throne.

Of all the royal daughters I was often judged the most beautiful. I should have been a prize in the marriage market. But I was also considered odd, unfeminine, which was probably why the suitor Laodice had nicknamed Old Coroebus was having such trouble making up his mind.

Coroebus, a prince from Bithynia, had visited four times in the past year. This time he brought me a silver distaff and two gold-embroidered robes from Scythia. For more than a week he sat in the main hall, casting sad, lovelorn looks in my direction whenever I passed by. This afternoon he had ridden off in his bronze chariot without having made an offer.

I had been enormously relieved. I had no wish to be bargained off in order to strengthen alliances with the northern kingdoms. But my sisters were never going to understand that.

"He'll be back," Laodice said, nodding solemnly.

"Up, both of you! Back to bed." I grabbed a cloak and picked up my oil lamp. "Believe it or not, there are worse problems in the world than reluctant suitors!"

And there was only one person in Troy I could talk to about them. The other strange one in our family was my twin brother, Helenus. He too had the "sight." As soon as I ushered my sisters back to their room across the hall, I ran to tell him about my vision.

CHAPTER TWO

⤙✦⤚

He was awake, black curls sleep-tossed, smiling his half smile. I knew he would be waiting for me. We were that attuned, my twin and I, two halves of the same soul. "Come, tell me," he said, patting the place next to him on the couch, and then, "How's the headache?"

"Going away." I sat rubbing my temples, listening to my heart pound. I didn't know how to make him feel the urgency. "You were right about Paris," I said, "about his 'trade delegation.'"

Over a year ago, when Paris proposed sailing to the Greek mainland, Helenus had warned the voyage would bring disaster. "Little good in being right," he said now. "Father commissioned Paris a ship of his own."

"A finer galley than even Hector sails." I sighed, remembering. Eldest son and pride of our nation, Hector had rightly suffered from this slight to his status. For weeks our large, quarrelsome family had argued over Paris's red ship, large enough for forty oarsmen, while Hector's galley accommodated only thirty-four.

People said Father had commissioned it out of guilt. Before Paris was born, an oracle predicted he would bring ruin to the house of Priam, so Father ordered the baby abandoned on the mountainside. The shepherd charged with this task, feeling pity for the well-formed male child, kept him for his own. But through a series of coincidences—and the luck of the goddess Aphrodite, whose favor my brother courted outrageously—Paris found his way back to the citadel fifteen years later. This time his true father and mother ignored the oracles and welcomed their son with open arms.

"I never understood why you opposed the voyage so bitterly," I said to Helenus. "I didn't want to tell you, but I was relieved to be getting rid of the royal seducer."

Helenus laughed. "Our nobles must be relieved too. They no longer have to worry about where their wives and concubines have disappeared to."

"But you were *right* about the voyage to Greece! The oracles were right! Paris should have been strangled at birth! Father should never have trusted the job to a peasant. . . ."

"Tell me what you saw."

I closed my eyes to recapture the images. "He's coming home, bringing a beautiful woman. Blonde, with flowers in her hair—and the sweetest smile." I described the flaming flute, the field of dying warriors. "She brings death to us. Is that what *you* saw?"

"Nothing so specific. Just a feeling in my bowels whenever Paris talked about trade opportunities with the Mycenaeans. He was lying. Our brother had other reasons for wanting to make that trip."

"He will destroy us. Through her." I shivered, and he put an arm around me. "How can I warn them?"

"You can't. Even *I* failed to keep Father from sending forth his golden-haired son in a vermillion galley, for all the world to see how glorious we are here in Troy. The gods will punish us for such arrogance. They always do."

"I'll go to Father myself. He *has* to remember the earth-quake, the year the harvest failed. Remember? I got them out of the temple before the roof beams fell. . . ."

"They thought a mountain lion was attacking you."

"I was shouting for them to get out of the building."

"*I* know that. But no matter how many events you pre-dict, *they'll* never believe you." Helenus smiled sadly. "Apollo's curse."

This was my brother's explanation for my poor reputa-tion as a seer. He liked to tease me about having won the love of the god Apollo, back when I was being trained in the secret temple rites. Not that either of us ever saw the god with our own eyes. Helenus's speculations were based on mysterious glowing lights that lingered beside me whenever I was in the holy shrine. My twin had wanted me to leave special sacrifices, or better yet, spend the night in the sanc-tuary alone. Helenus said Apollo had given me the gift of sight, but when I had refused his love, he had added a cruel condition: that my countrymen would never believe my predictions.

My mother had a different explanation for the visions. She said my twin and I had fallen asleep in Apollo's temple one day when our nurse went off to meet a lover. While we slept, sacred temple serpents came and licked our ears.

Neither explanation made sense. I don't remember falling

asleep inside the temple, and we never went near the sacred snakes, which were contained inside a pit in any event. And surely the great Apollo would have been more direct in his courtship.

Still, I knew why Helenus was so much more likely to be believed. A better judge of human nature, my brother knew when to keep his visions to himself. Except for that one occasion—warning Father not to let Paris set sail for Greece—Helenus only announced happy events.

I had frightened off my audience. I had wanted to save lives and harvests each time I learned they were doomed. But human nature is not very logical. My countrymen wanted none of my bad news, so they rejected whatever salvation my foreknowledge might have provided.

I had spent the last three years trying to be more like Helenus and less like myself. Now if I saw a fisherman setting out on a calm morning, and a vision flashed before my eyes of stormy seas and a boat dashed against rocks, I said nothing, painful as it was to keep silent. Ironically, I think this effort to stay out of people's affairs made me seem aloof, even more peculiar than before, when I was shouting my warnings. But tonight's dream was too important to keep to myself. "What can I do?" I asked Helenus.

"Nothing. You will never be believed, no matter what you do."

"We can't just *wait* for her to come!"

"We can *only* wait . . . and sacrifice to the gods who rule over our lives."

Sacrifices were always generous in Troy. King Priam was famous as a man who offered the best ten-year-old oxen, the most precious Rhodian wine to the gods and goddesses who protect our great city. He even remembered those members of the heavenly family who had little interest is us or who, like gray-eyed Athena, were committed to Greek cities.

And we had powerful supporters of our own on Mount Olympus. Zeus, for example, had a special fondness for the house of Priam. Everyone knew that Troy's prosperity as well as Priam's success at siring sons were due to the great god's patronage. Father's wives and concubines—accumulated through a lifetime of alliances and conquests—gave him political stature. His fine horses showed the world our military might. Priam wore his royal dignity whether he romped in the courtyard with his children or presided over the Council of Elders, listening with courtesy to even the most bombastic of ministers. Phoenician traders, made to pay dearly for the privilege of passing through our straits, went away admiring the great Trojan king. In other ports they praised his banquets and hunts, the valor of his sons, the beauty of his daughters. Father basked in this reflection of himself. He enjoyed his own righteousness.

Some citizens grumbled about the time spent in temples, the prize oxen that could have been used for breeding purposes. After all, they argued, there was little to threaten our lives, other than vague rumors of a war with the Greeks, the stuff of songs and legends. Our people had grown used to such stories.

But I continued to brood over the connection between that great war and my dream, to agonize over my own helplessness.

"Can't I go to Father? Tell him about the dream?" I

asked Helenus over and over again during those months of waiting.

"What would you tell him?" my brother would respond. "Is it such surprising news that Paris has a beautiful blonde on board his galley? We don't even know her name."

It was more than a year before we learned who she was, and by then it was too late to do anything about her. She was called Helen of Sparta, but her name would soon be linked forever with that of our city. Helen was part of that great war the legends foretold, woven into the same fateful strand. And she was sailing toward us, along with our destiny.

CHAPTER THREE

❧

News of her came in early spring, from Phoenician traders stopping to exchange wine and hides for horses and corn. One of them was brought to the palace to tell Father what he knew. The man was fair-skinned for a Phoenician and had a scar that took away part of his lower lip.

"I saw them myself, your son and Helen of Sparta," he said. "In Cyprus at the Temple of Aphrodite. The stories are true; she's a goddess among women." He told Father how Helen had run away with Paris the preceding autumn, taking most of the palace treasury with her on board his ship. The Phoenician called it an elopement and made jokes about the jilted husband, King Menelaus.

The Greek delegation that arrived a month later called it a kidnapping, and to them it was no laughing matter. According to their version of the story, Paris stole Helen while her husband was away attending a kinsman's funeral.

Menelaus was well connected. He was younger brother to Agamemnon, High King over all Greece and leader of the Greek Confederacy. To retrieve Helen and her treasure, the Greeks sent King Nestor of Pylos and Odysseus of Ithaca, along with a company of lesser nobles. Father received them with the usual pomp.

The Greeks presented their case at an emergency meeting of the Council of Elders. At first talk was cordial, the two sides feeling each other out, but Greek tempers soon flared. When Nestor called Paris a "curly-haired wife snatcher," I exchanged glances with my twin, who sat beside me in the gallery.

I had walked in right behind him. There were some raised eyebrows, which I pretended not to notice, but no one dared challenge my presence. Although Mother attended council sessions on ceremonial occasions, none of the other women had penetrated this male ritual. Earlier that morning I had tried to persuade my mother and Andromache, my brother Hector's wife, to come with me. They had declined, of course, and Andromache had reminded me that women weren't *supposed* to be interested in matters of state.

I hadn't wasted time arguing. I left them in the women's quarters with their weaving. They would be interested enough when their sons and husbands were falling under Greek swords. Already there were rumors of war if Helen were not immediately returned to her husband, and we didn't even know where she and Paris were. I, for one, refused to hear about these negotiations secondhand.

Seated on his throne, Father presided over the debate. A tall figure in a gold-trimmed robe, with silver hair and the slightly slanted blue eyes Paris had inherited, Priam looked every bit the great king. He listened without interruption to Nestor's long-winded oration.

When the elderly Greek finally finished, Father pointed out, in the most cordial of tones, that kidnapping was perhaps not an accurate term. "After all," he continued, "Paris took with him only a small band of warriors. He could not have removed Helen and her treasure against her will."

"What about the forty oarsmen?" I whispered to Helenus.

"Shh! Odysseus is about to speak. Besides, that's not the point. Paris wouldn't have needed to use force. Everyone knows that."

Odysseus had a stern expression, hair the color of hay, and shoulders too wide for his height. Wearing the plain, unbleached tunic of peasants and farmers, he did not command respect until he began to speak. Then his deep voice and richly embellished phrases claimed our full attention.

"You may call Helen's departure whatever you wish," he said. "The fact remains that for Paris to have taken her—with or without her cooperation—was an unpardonable breach of the laws of hospitality. Those very laws that separate us in the civilized world from the barbarians that encircle us. . . ."

He looked pointedly at Father, and our elders shifted in their seats. Rigid laws define the rights and responsibilities of visitors to royal households. Guests, no matter how unwelcome, are completely safe inside an enemy citadel. Their hosts would never harm them. It is just as unthinkable for visitors to steal from their hosts.

"Odysseus is right," Helenus whispered. "Civilized men agree to live by rules whenever they travel from home. Paris has broken those rules."

We Trojans wanted desperately to be thought of as civilized. And Father believed his reign had placed us among the civilized, that Troy alone among Asian kingdoms had somehow earned this status. For Priam, the only unpardonable insult was "barbarian."

"I have no knowledge of my son's whereabouts," Father finally said. "He is apparently in no hurry to get home. We heard recently he had raided the city of Sidon."

The Greeks exchanged veiled looks.

"He's picked up three more ships and a full company of warriors in Cyprus," Father explained. "But as soon as he returns, I will see to it that Paris rectifies this act of bad faith. You can tell Menelaus I have no wish to deprive him of his lawful wife."

After Father dismissed the council, my brother and I had little time to talk. Mother was frantic with preparations for a banquet to honor our guests. She needed me to direct the servants, who were scurrying up and down stairs responding to shouted demands, baskets of grain and jugs of wine perched precariously on their heads. I had to make sure they mixed the wine in the proper proportions, three parts water to one part wine. Only barbarians drank unmixed wine; Mother was afraid too strong a batch might slip by and dishonor us.

In the aftermath of the deliberations a holiday mood had swept our city. My brothers Hector and Deiphobus had taken our visitors on a tour of the royal stables. Hector, whose nickname was Tamer of Horses, would entertain them with a display of horsemanship, followed by chariot races. It was rumored that Father would offer a champion stallion to each of the Greek kings.

"He's going to make Paris send her back," I said to Helenus, breathless with relief. "Wasn't it brilliant the way Odysseus trapped Father in that breach of hospitality argument?"

Slaves sat crouched in the shade of the veranda grinding barley in hand mills to make bread for our feast and laughing among themselves. Even they seemed relieved that the great war had been turned away from our gates.

But Helenus shook his head. "I'm not sure." He closed his eyes, turning inward. He was so still he seemed not to be breathing. "I don't see anything," he said.

"Nor do I! Let's accept that as a good omen." I seized his hands. "Brother, we've carried this vision of doom in our hearts for more than a year. Let's allow ourselves to rejoice!"

I left him then and went in search of myrtle leaves and white narcissus to weave a head garland for Odysseus. Later that afternoon Father presented the stallions, and at the banquet that night even the dour Odysseus sat smiling—and wearing the garland I had made for him. Helenus told me later that during the drinking Odysseus had said that he, too, was relieved, that Helen was not worth a war.

We women did not attend the feast. It was known that in Greece noblewomen attended state banquets. In Troy such free association between the sexes was frowned upon. Still, I was there on the sidelines, making sure the wine was properly mixed, listening to the bards, watching the jugglers tossing and catching plates, doing their handstands to entertain the warriors. And I felt as if a great weight had been lifted from me.

But my rejoicing was short-lived. The following week my suitor Coroebus returned to Troy with a solid gold armband and the offer of a bride-price for me. And before I could learn how dowry negotiations were going down in the men's hall, a second suitor appeared on the scene!

His name was Othronus. He was crown prince of Cabesus, a mountainous kingdom far to the north in Thracian territory. He had traveled to Troy after hearing prophecies of a great war with Greece in which he sought to distinguish himself. Seeing me and the wealth of our citadel, he hurried to match Coroebus's offer.

Both suitors remained after the Greek delegation left, and nightly feasting continued in the great hall. In the hushed seclusion of the women's quarters servants whispered over the latest bride-price offers, while my sisters Polyxena and Laodice made wicked comparisons of the two suitors, watching me closely for any reaction.

"Two handsome warriors fighting to have you," my mother said one morning. "You could at least say a word of greeting to them."

"Fighting for *me* or for the political advantages of a union with Troy?"

"For both, of course! What peculiar questions you ask, Cassandra."

It was no use explaining how I felt—she would never understand—or begging for help, which she would have been quite powerless to give. Instead, I climbed the hill to the temples and prayed for divine intervention, offering sacrifices to all the gods. After days of agonizing over each new rumor, I told Helenus I had decided to become a temple virgin, sworn to remain chaste in service to the great Apollo.

"You don't want to do that." Helenus shook his head, laughing. "The priests would be even worse than a husband! You'd hate it! The truth is, negotiations have stalled. I think 'Old' Coroebus is secretly scared to death of you. He hasn't matched the Thracian's bride-price. Still, Othronus has little to offer politically. Of course, Father is enjoying the bargaining for its own sake. It's better sport than boar hunting. . . ."

"I refuse to be bargained off! I'll run away!" I cried, jumping up from my chair. "I'll disguise myself as a man! Oh, why wasn't I *born* a man?"

"You think it's so easy to be a man?"

"At least *you* have choices!"

"Not so many as you think. Father is still set on that Phoenician widow for me, one of the barbarians. I've never even seen her. Besides," he said, mimicking Andromache, "*you're* not *supposed* to want choices." He stopped smiling then and sat looking up at me in silence. "Poor Cassandra," he said softly, "so out of fit with the world you were born into."

I sank into the chair beside him. "I'd rather die than marry either of them."

"You won't have to," he said after another silence.

"What have you seen? Tell me!"

But he didn't explain. "Just let yourself enjoy the attention," he said, and then, "It won't hurt you to understand it better, this marriage market, as you call it. This women's world you're so reluctant to join."

"It wouldn't be fair to give them false hopes."

"Neither courtship will come to anything. Believe me."

I looked up the hill at Apollo's temple, bone white in the sun's glare. It seemed more a prison than a haven.

"Coroebus is a taciturn sort," Helenus went on. "But Othronus is a good lad—and he's utterly smitten by your dark beauty. It won't hurt you to be kind to him. Do it as a favor to me."

"You're certain I won't have to follow him to a land of snow and ice and fiery volcanos?"

"Certain."

"Laodice and Polyxena have picked him as their favorite too," I said, smiling, feeling a sudden need to lighten my brother's spirits. His eyes looked to sad.

I trusted Helenus completely. I took his advice.

Othronus was tall and sandy-haired. He spoke no Greek and little Lycian, our Trojan language. Our conversations were accomplished with gestures and laughter. He would run to catch up whenever he saw me passing through the main courtyard and arrive by my side breathless and speechless, blushing furiously as his retainers shouted encouragement in their strange, singsong tongue.

"Have you started learning Thracian?" my brother Hector asked me one morning in a teasing voice. On his way to the stables Hector had just observed one of these "chance" meetings.

I pointed to the somewhat wilted roses Othronus had thrust into my hands. "*Louvia*," I said. "I'm assuming it means 'flowers.'"

"He's a sturdy lad and a fine horseman. Still, I hope you will trust us to make the best decision on your behalf."

"Have no fear, my lord, there will be no more elopements in our family."

Hector didn't pick up on the sarcasm in my voice. He smiled and patted my shoulder with his huge hand, "Well spoken, girl. I should have known that your head will always rule over your heart."

I felt guilty about my flippant remark. Taller than Paris, with the same fine features, Hector was in fact a larger, darker imprint of our now world-famous second brother. He was also as noble and kind as Paris was selfish and mean-spirited. He had been watching me closely, and it occurred to me that he probably planned to throw his weight in Othronus's direction, despite the territorial advantages of a union with Coroebus. I had indeed learned something about the marriage market. There were men, like Hector, who cared more about a sister's happiness, as he understood it, than political advantages.

I began to enjoy the courtship ritual, to sit back and watch the diplomatic moves and analyze them with my twin, to giggle with Laodice and Polyxena over Othronus's endearing attempts to make an impression. I remember those weeks as a time of silly jokes and long evenings that deepened into starry nights and dreamless sleep.

And then, one morning, this happy interlude ended.

The vision came without warning. I was passing a row of chariots in the outer court when two currents of pain started at the back of my neck and surged upward to my temples.

I was running through the same field of writhing bodies I had seen in my dream. But now, at my feet, lay my brother Hector, his naked body gashed and bruised, his hair plastered with blood. Face down, he was sprawled in the mud behind a bronze chariot, finer than any I'd ever seen, its gold trimmings flashing in the sun.

I ran toward the men's court, the place of formal greetings. I knew she would be there—Helen of Sparta.

A dozen or so of my brothers and as many other nobles were gathered. I didn't even look to see if Helenus was among them. Father had risen from his throne and was approaching Paris and his Greek conquest, the woman from my dream.

Throwing myself at his feet, I shouted my warning. "Beware the whore of Sparta! Send her back to her husband or we will live to see our men slaughtered, our children tossed from the walls, our women carried off as slaves. . . ."

Father lifted me to my feet, frowning to silence me, visibly embarrassed. I, too, was suddenly embarrassed by my loss of control. I had promised myself I would never again give way to such hysteria, no matter how urgent the message.

The pain in my temples was subsiding, and I felt the physical relief wash over me, as it always did after a vision. No one spoke. It was so quiet I could hear them breathing. My brothers looked from me to Helen; her eyes were fixed on me.

She wore a robe the soft purple color of wild hyacinth and a silver anklet in the shape of a coiled snake. She held tight to Paris's hand, her astonished eyes bluer than any blue I'd ever seen. Spartan women are supposed to be tough, but there was a softness about her that made me want to protect her—though she was my elder by at least a year and my mortal enemy as well.

I don't know how long we stood there before Mother came and took hold of me. My legs still numb and tingling, I let myself be led back into the crowd.

Father delivered the formal greeting. Then Helen placed her small, white hand in his. He was enchanted by her, as were all the men who had come to reprimand Paris for this reckless deed.

She was the female counterpart of my beautiful brother. The two were fashioned of the same elements, gold and lapis and ivory. To see them standing together seemed right. All of us felt that.

It was too late to turn back our destiny. Instead of sending her back to Menelaus, Troy opened its hearts and its gates to her.

CHAPTER FOUR

❧

F ather was delighted with Paris's contributions to
our royal treasury, bronze tripods and silver bowls
from the sack of Sidon, gold and jewelry taken from
Sparta. Predictably, Hector disapproved of Paris's garnet
earrings, the same ones I had seen in my dream. They had
been part of Helen's dowry. Hector called them "Persian
foolery," and Father made jokes about this new male
fashion, but within a week six of the younger brothers were
wearing earrings of their own.

The men of our family, especially the younger brothers
and half brothers, were happy to have Paris back. He
was, after all, one of ours, and excellent company in the
men's hall, a singer of songs and teller of tales. Witty and
irreverent, Paris also knew how to make jokes about himself. And even though their handsome nemesis had
returned, our nobles no longer had to worry about straying
concubines. Paris was content to spend all his nights with
Helen.

I would have expected our women to be jealous of this
radiant blonde. But they were charmed by her at first. Even

I, knowing what I knew, felt drawn to her. Helen's beauty was more than physical. It went deeper. The shepherds have an expression for it, for that occasional sheep that is so gentle the others in the flock become gentle in its presence. "Bone sweet," they call it. That was Helen, bone sweet. She believed the best in people, and they responded in kind. Sometimes I caught myself wishing I could be like her, instead of always analyzing hidden motives and distancing myself from people.

Her upturned face, full of mirth and trust, brightened our days as she shared her stories and her beauty secrets. My sisters were soon tinting their cheeks with alkanet juice and styling their hair with a device called a curling iron that Helen had brought from Greece. This wood-handled rod was warmed on a brazier and used to twist strands of hair into ringlets.

About a month after her arrival I found Helen in the women's courtyard performing this operation on my sister Polyxena, while my youngest sister Laodice watched with round eyes. "Careful," Helen said to Polyxena. "You must stand very still so that I don't burn your pretty face."

Polyxena obeyed, eyes squeezed closed. Helen, who was using her left hand to shield Polyxena's forehead, glanced up and saw me and quickly lowered her eyes. No doubt she was unsure of what to expect, although I had given no warnings since that first day. I stood watching, knowing I had dampened her spirits and that my two favorite sisters would be relieved when I left.

I envied their easy closeness. I was jealous of the way Laodice liked to curl up in Helen's lap. I had no female friends. Women were wary of me. Of all my sisters and half sisters, only these two youngest somehow managed to accept me, and I worried that as they grew into women they, too, would become strangers. Not that I had ever really tried reaching out to the others. So much of what women did together struck me as falsehood and foolishness. Yet as I stood there, part of me longed for Helen to offer to curl my hair too.

Transformed by curly bangs, Polyxena twirled around in front of me. "Cassandra, look! It's an Athenian *coiffure*. Helen learned how to do it in *Athens*! When she was *kidnapped* by Theseus! She was only twelve years old! Younger than *me*!"

"You mustn't bother Cassandra with my gossip," Helen said as she wrapped the curling iron in a towel, preparing to leave. In the weeks since her arrival she'd hastened to get out of my way each time I came upon her, quickly returning to Paris's apartments on the northern side of the great hall. My sisters found frequent excuses to spend time with her there. Even my mother and Hector's very proper wife, Andromache, had visited twice, returning to their rooms with ringlets framing their faces.

"Stay," I said to her now. "I just came to tell you the news. We've received word that the Greek delegation is returning."

She dropped into a chair, her face pale. "How do you know?"

"Merchants from Crete. They've seen the Greek forces gathering on the coast, at Aulis. In case Father refuses to give you up."

"Almighty Zeus," she said, reaching for Polyxena's hand. "What will happen to us?"

I wanted to ask why she hadn't worried about that when she ran off with my brother. "They're getting ready to attack," I said instead. "A thousand ships. All the suitors who swore the Oath of the Horse and many others who begrudge us our prosperity."

The oath had become a favorite subject of speculation here in Troy. Even six-year-old Laodice knew how twelve Greek kings had sworn to avenge Helen's chosen husband in case she were stolen from him. I wondered if these warriors ever dreamed the threat would come from across the sea—and that it would give them an excuse to attack our wealthy city and remove our treasures, just as Paris had done in Sparta.

"They're sending Nestor and Odysseus . . . to negotiate your release," I added. "And your husband, Menelaus."

"Immortal gods! *I cannot face him!*" She covered her face with her hands, and Polyxena knelt beside her to offer comfort.

I found myself regretting my words. I should have let Mother bring the news; she would have done it more gracefully. Anyone who had seen Helen with my brother Paris knew she didn't want to be released. But the decision to give Helen back to her husband was my father's to make. It was Priam who had the power to cancel this war, not Helen. As a woman, she would do as she was told. Besides, from all accounts of their military preparations the Greek Confederacy didn't seem very eager to avoid bloodshed.

"Don't blame yourself," I said. "You've given your countrymen an honorable excuse to do something they've wanted to for some time."

She looked up, eyes brimming.

"This is also a dispute about trade," I explained to Laodice and Polyxena. "The Greeks want to import their corn from Asia Minor without having to pay for passing through our straits."

"If the Greeks want war, we'll give it to them," Polyxena cried. "Hector will send them running in terror!"

Laodice said, "Helen's not a slave, she's a *queen*. Can't she live where she pleases?"

Helen and I smiled sadly at each other; I shook my head.

"*Can't* she?" Laodice pleaded.

"Would that this were so," I said.

"Why not?"

"She just can't, that's all! There doesn't have to be a reason! That's just the way things are."

I felt the familiar anger rising in my chest. Not wanting to vent it on poor Laodice, I made some excuse and hurried to leave the courtyard. How could I explain the powerlessness of our sex in words my six-year-old sister could understand? Laodice would have to live in this world of men. What advice could I give her when I didn't know how to live in it myself? And yet she had helped me see Helen's actions in a new light. Why shouldn't a queen have the same rights to her body and property as a king? Helen's escape from Menelaus wasn't so different from my own resistance to being bartered in marriage to the prince of a neighboring kingdom.

The Greeks sent the same kings as before, perhaps counting upon the respect we had shared during the first visit. But this time even Odysseus's eloquence was powerless to sway Father's decision. And it made matters worse to have the stocky, bandy-legged Menelaus along, shouting insults at the Council of Elders and glaring over at Paris with eyes like hot coals.

We received almost daily accounts of the Greek buildup at Aulis. In spite of the initial cordiality of Odysseus and Nestor, the Greeks were apparently preparing for a war they believed inevitable. Discussions soon took the form of ultimatums.

"Are you threatening war if we do not hand over Queen Helen?" Father asked Nestor at the second of two meetings. Paris, seated to Priam's right, clenched his fists.

Nestor answered, "Agamemnon's patience is wearing thin. His brother—Menelaus here—has been gravely wronged. A wrong, I remind you, that *you* promised to right."

Menelaus fumed silently, staring at Paris with such naked hatred that people averted their eyes.

"Our curly-headed wife snatcher wouldn't survive two minutes in his clutches," I whispered to Helenus.

I had again slipped into the gallery along with my twin. This time Mother and Andromache had decided to attend the proceedings, hiding behind their veils at the back of the room. Helen had remained in Paris's quarters under guard. It was good she had been spared this look on her husband's face.

As the afternoon wore on, Odysseus spoke of Priam's promise to return Helen to her lawful husband. But these reminders worked against the Greek cause. The clever Odysseus could not have known it, but Father would do almost anything to avoid seeing himself in the wrong.

So Priam became defensive, accusing the Greeks of

inventing an excuse to wage war against Troy, insisting, just as his six-year-old daughter had done a week before, that Helen had a right to choose where she wanted to live—and with whom.

Even the Trojans recognized this claim as false. "Not so!" Helenus said into my ear. "A moral law dictates that a woman may not leave her husband for another man, even a man who looks like our brother Paris."

"But *why* does that have to be?"

He smiled his half smile. "Haven't we worn out this subject? Because, my dear, reasonable Cassandra, men make the laws. And they don't want their wives running off with men who look like Paris."

A merchant named Antimachus had jumped to his feet and was shaking his fist at the Greeks. "We Trojans will not be bullied," he shouted. "Helen stays here!"

In the din that followed, Helenus leaned over and said, "I wonder how much Paris had to pay for this heroic declaration."

Everyone knew Antimachus's vote—or witness—was for sale. Still, none of our elders dared speak against him. Truth to tell, they were all enchanted by Helen, and our warriors had begun to relish the taste of battle, like blood on their tongues.

Antimachus was shouting again. "We'll have no more of your threats! Troy has powerful allies to rally in this fight!" He pointed his spear at Menelaus. "We could kill you right here! Leave Helen a widow, free to dispose of herself and her property at will! And no one in this assembly has any doubt what her choice would be."

Menelaus had gone rigid. Odysseus kept a restraining hand on his shoulder to stop him from drawing his sword.

"Go gather your army!" Antimachus shouted. "She's *ours* now! For all time! Helen of *Troy*!"

I reached for my brother's hand and held it tightly while the Greeks stomped out of the hall.

CHAPTER FIVE

❧

A few noblemen grumbled about Paris's purchase of support from Antimachus. Some others recalled the prophecy connecting Paris's birth with the sack of our city—and wished he had died on the mountainside. And a growing number of women blamed Helen in advance for the battle deaths of their husbands. Most passionate among these potential widows was Hector's wife, Andromache, who was pregnant with their first child. Andromache knew that Hector, as commander of Trojan forces, would be a choice target for Greek bowmen.

Hector did not share his wife's prejudices. While he had no love for our brother Paris, Hector saw Helen as a helpless woman in a strange land, and therefore beyond reproach. Of course Andromache never expressed her opinions outside of the women's quarters. Andromache was a model wife. Her meekness and obedience had always annoyed me. But Hector had to see the poison in his wife's eyes whenever she came upon "our Greek treasure," as women had begun to call Helen, with bitter sarcasm.

So on the eve of war Troy's people stood divided. Like

Father, most of the men still adored Helen. And for him, these months had brought an excitement he must have missed in his peaceful old age. He dispatched spies, disguised as Phoenician merchants, to the port of Aulis. They reported back on the gathering of Greek clans, which grew larger each day. Mulling over their reports, Father planned our defense in endless conversations with the elders, his eyes sparkling with the strategic challenge of choosing battle sites and positioning men to combat a force that would greatly outnumber our own. All the old men had stories of their own bravery against impossible odds. Clearly, they missed those days of battle.

As the Greeks waited for favorable winds, my brothers sailed their galleys up the Bosphorus into the Black Sea, forging alliances with Thracian kingdoms eager for the glory of battle and a share of the Greeks' precious metals and slaves.

Helenus's prediction held true. Both my suitors offered to join the fight, and still Father postponed a decision, claiming this was not a time for celebrating weddings, but for combating the Greek threat to Asia Minor. To compete for Priam's favor, both Coroebus and Othronus agreed to return home and raise armies. Coroebus, apparently paralyzed by his shyness, left Troy without a word to me.

Othronus left on the seventh day of the month of the first harvest, a holy day sacred to Apollo. The morning of his departure Othronus found me on the staircase that led to the Temple of Apollo, on my way to offer sacrifices. He handed me another of his bouquets, this one of wild daisies picked on the hillside. He'd learned enough of our language to tell me he would return with "many man and horses" and to ask me to pray for his victory in battle. He still blushed in my presence.

I took both his hands and wished him safe return, praying with all my heart that I would be spared any fore-knowledge of what would become of him. We stood a moment on the staircase, the sun gilding his fair hair. Then I watched him lope down the rocky trail to where his men waited, his red cape flying behind him, the thrill of the journey, of future skirmishes, in every bound.

I felt a pang of fear. I didn't want to know if he would gain the recognition he longed for as a warrior, if he would even survive the war. This morning I planned to pray to the great Apollo not for the survival of my city, but for something much simpler—for a release from further visions.

"Will he be back?" Helen asked me a moment later. She had passed Othronus on her way up to the temple. "What do you see for his future?" she said when I appeared not to understand her question.

I studied her expression. She was not making fun of me. "I don't know," I said. "I don't want to know."

"How do you live with it? Your gift."

"I try to ignore it."

"It hurts, doesn't it, having a vision?"

Instinctively, my hands went up to my temples.

"You were holding your head like that . . . the day I arrived."

"It's like going inside a tunnel of pain. Headfirst. Worse than the pain is the *knowing*." I shook my head. "Much worse. I was just standing here thinking of how I could ask Apollo to take back his gift."

"I've heard about the sacred snakes. From your mother."

"If that story is true, the snake that licked my brother's ears did a better job. No one believes me."

"What do the visions look like?"

"Like memories. Memories of the future."

"And you saw *me* in one?"

I looked down at Othronus's daisies. I no longer wanted to hurt her.

"Tell me." She sat on the bottom step, shielding her eyes from the sun. "Please!"

She wore a plain white robe in reverence to the gods. Her pale hair was pulled into a simple knot at the base of her neck, just as I wore my dark brown hair. Even with no ringlets, no rouge on her cheeks, she was breathtaking.

"You're better off not knowing," I said. But when she continued to look up at me with pleading eyes, I sat down beside her, the flowers in my lap. I told her about my dream, about Paris's garnet earrings and the silver flute, about the field of dying warriors, about Hector lying dead behind the gold-trimmed chariot.

"Would that I had never been born," she said softly. She frowned up at the columns that fronted the first of the temples. "I had no power to refuse him. I left my child, my country, my life." Helen's sweet face begged for understanding. "It was the work of the goddess Aphrodite," she said.

I nodded. She was far too soft to have resisted a man like Paris.

"Can this . . . memory ever be changed?" she asked. "Oracles on both sides of the Aegean have been predicting this war for years."

"That's the question I'm always asking Helenus. He thinks the gods do sometimes hold out a chance to us." I picked petals off one of the daisies. "My father could decide to send you back."

"Sometimes I wish he would."

Andromache chose that moment to pass by on her way up to the temple, acknowledging me with a nod and casting her venomous glance at Helen, who shivered in the full sunlight.

"She's a silly woman," I said after Andromache was out of earshot. "She thinks it's you she hates, but it's really the *thought* of losing Hector. She has no interest in anything else. World events are reduced to one issue: will Hector live or die? It must be pleasant to be so single-minded."

"Not always," Helen whispered. Clearly, she understood such single-mindedness better than I.

"Andromache and her friends are just women," I said. "But if enough *men* turned against you, there would be no war."

"Perhaps a compromise could be reached?" Helen suggested timidly. "If Menelaus would accept the treasure instead. If Paris offered to return it?"

It didn't seem likely that my brother would agree to give back the gold and silver Helen had added to our royal treasury, but I didn't want to burden her with this thought. "Perhaps it's out of our hands," I said. "You say you could not refuse Paris, in spite of the consequences. I believe you." I pointed at Andromache. In her sixth month of pregnancy, she was making her way laboriously up the steep staircase. "Her child will be stillborn," I said. "There's no point in warning her—even if she would believe me, and she wouldn't—because there's nothing she can do to prevent it."

Helen's sapphire blue eyes were fixed on my face.

"Sometimes there's nothing we can do to save ourselves," I said. "But if the gods hold out a chance, it's because the gods love a good joke."

I picked up my flowers and stood, shaking petals off my skirt. Then, turning back, I glanced up at Andromache. "Mind you," I said, "she will hate you even more after that."

CHAPTER SIX

That autumn Andromache's son was born dead the same week the Greek fleet set sail from Aulis. My mother was able to stop her daughter-in-law's bleeding with sacred herbs, and we women built a pyre and burned the body on the hill above the palace, where funeral services for unnamed children were performed. Scraping the earth with our garden tools, we built a mound over the ashes and tiny, pitiful bones.

Andromache wept bitterly as she watched us work. "Hector should be here to cover the ashes, pour the libations," she kept saying.

"We're better than house servants," I snapped at one point in the endless afternoon.

"Have no fear," my mother said gently, shooting me a look of reproach. "Your son will be able to make his journey to the Land of the Dead. The rituals have been accomplished correctly."

I didn't argue with her, but this was not true. Hector should have been there, or at least one of the full brothers. Cremation rituals had to be performed by a family's top-ranking nobleman, but all our men were away cementing alliances with the Thracians or preparing a camp in the foothills.

In the women's quarters we could only wait. Skies over Troy were dark. Thunder rumbled down from Mount Ida; tempers flared over inconsequential things. A lady's maid unlucky enough to step on the hem of Andromache's robe was slapped hard and banished to the kitchens.

When we heard from Father's spies that the great fleet had sailed, we prayed for a hurricane to sink the thousand ships and thousands of Greek warriors.

But no storm came, only a blanket of clouds that blocked out the sun. Some called it a sign that Zeus had withdrawn his protection from our city.

For a time, the previous summer, it had seemed that the Greek fleet would never sail for Troy. We heard stories of infighting within the Greek coalition, while their men waited for the summer winds that would propel their ships across the Aegean to our coasts. But no winds came. Not a leaf stirred.

For two months the thousand ships had sat becalmed in the Bay of Aulis. Sun beat down on the tents. Food supplies ran low, we were told, and springs dried up. Patience wore thin. Warriors from all over the Greek mainland and the scattered islands fought with each other, establishing rivalries that would outlast the war.

Finally, in early autumn, Agamemnon consulted an oracle who told him he would have to sacrifice his daughter Iphigenia, his firstborn and favorite child, to bring about the westerly winds and prevent the Greeks from waging war among themselves.

This news, relayed by our network of spies, arrived several days after we heard about the sailing. Helen learned of it first. "My niece Iphigenia—my first victim!" she cried. We were huddled together with Laodice and Polyxena trying to keep warm in the chill dampness of the women's quarters, trying to make sense of this event.

"Agamemnon made up a story to get my sister Clytemnestra to bring their daughter down to Aulis," Helen explained. "He told her Iphigenia was to be married to the great Achilles! Told her that Achilles refused to sail for Troy until they were married. So my sister brought Iphigenia to their camp—a radiant girl, glowing with pride at the honor. And her father, Agamemnon, waited, and with him a priest, holding the knife that would slit her throat."

Everyone knew Achilles was the greatest warrior on earth. Some prophecies claimed that without him the Greeks would never triumph over Troy. Our informants didn't know if the young hero had participated in this terrible deception. Some said he'd protested to Agamemnon, tried to warn the girl, offered her his protection. Already a story had begun to circulate that the goddess Artemis carried the victim up to Mount Olympus before the knife ever touched her throat.

In the women's quarters, hugging our knees, we speculated endlessly about whether Iphigenia had struggled with the priests. A sacrificial animal has to make its own way to the stone altar without being dragged or even led. But a daughter! We had no models for such a sacrifice, no way to imagine it. Had she clung to her mother? Had she screamed and pleaded for her life at Agamemnon's knees?

"He's a monster," Helen said. "My sister should have poisoned his wine."

"I was thinking about that," I said. "We don't know how much time she had, after she learned the truth of that summons to Aulis." I studied Helen's face, shocked at her fury. Of all the women I'd known, Helen was least likely to think of poisoning anyone. She was beginning to sound like me. Had I been Clytemnestra, *I* would have found some way to poison his wine.

Somehow during those weeks I had come to be Helen's confidante. She missed her daughter desperately and lavished affection on my younger sisters, especially Laodice, who was not much older than Hermione. Since my twin, Helenus, was off preparing for war, I spent most of my time with these two sisters. Paris, too, was off training horses, assembling weapons, negotiating with allies. So Helen and I were thrown together often.

As we waited for the Greek fleet, I began to think of myself as her protector as well. Because I lived estranged from most members of my own family, I knew how Helen felt when Andromache passed her silently in the corridors, when my mother gave her tight-lipped greeting. Still, I was better prepared for such isolation. With her golden looks and sunny disposition Helen had never learned how to be an outcast.

"Why don't you hate me? Like the other women?" she asked me one afternoon after our men had returned. "Your brother Helenus will not escape the fighting, and you love him as much as any woman loves her husband."

We were sitting on a thick fleece, watching the autumn wine making. Helen had just given up trying to teach me a silly women's game called knucklebones, played with five tiny bones you were supposed to toss up and catch on the back of your hand. My brother Helenus stood next to one of the huge barrels that held the grapes, lifting Laodice so that she could see inside, where servants were trampling grapes as they danced, their feet and legs stained purple. A house slave named Metos played the lyre.

Shaking my head, I considered Helen's question. I *had* accepted the certainty that my twin would fight the Greeks, yet I felt no fear for his safety. "He will survive," I said. "I'm sure of it."

Holding Polyxena by the hand and still carrying Laodice, Helenus was leading a line dance in a circle around the three barrels. "Helenus knows it too," I said after a moment of silence.

"Another vision?"

"No, Apollo has been kind to me in that. Just a feeling, a very strong one."

"Some oracles are predicting the death of Hector on the field of battle. No wonder Andromache despises me."

I suppressed an image of Hector's mutilated body. "He'll have to face Achilles," I said softly.

Everyone knew that Achilles carried the god's protection like an invisible cloak. Arrows bounced off his back; iron swords broke against his muscled thighs—or so the stories went. When he entered the field of battle, keening his eerie war cry, the enemy panicked. The lust for slaughter in his eyes made men want to throw down their spears and surrender into his arms.

"But Achilles will not survive either," Helen went on. "That's another prophecy. Achilles had the choice of two destinies. He could live a long, peaceful life and die unknown, or he could fight in the Trojan War and earn eternal glory. Perhaps Hector will kill *him*."

"Who can tell? Oracles can be wrong," I said, praying that this would come true.

"Let's not talk about it anymore," she said, and reached for her flute. "We're supposed to be celebrating."

Even as we waited for the Greek fleet, the traditional week of wine making had brought a holiday mood, like a final feast before a fast. Our men had returned to the citadel. Our skies had miraculously cleared. Rays of sunshine projected patterns of fast-drifting clouds across the rolling plain. The drinking and merrymaking in the outer bailey had erupted even earlier than usual. We women had put on our finest robes, with wreaths of roses in our hair, and gone down to join the men.

Helen had curled my bangs with her iron, but I insisted on keeping the rest of my hair in the usual twist at the nape of my neck. She looked at me appraisingly during one of the breaks in the music. "All you need now is a little soot on your eyebrows . . . and some alkanet juice on your cheeks," she said. "Highlight those wonderful cheekbones."

"I told you, I don't want to look like a concubine!"

"You sound just like Andromache," Helen said, laughing, and then, as I was rousing myself to protest, "Look! Metos has dropped his lyre! Where is he—where are they all rushing to?"

Musicians and dancers were running toward the outer walls, servants climbing from wine vats, their purple feet staining the dry earth.

"The Greek fleet!" Helenus yelled to us. He set down Laodice so as to make better time and ran off.

I dashed after him. Polyxena and Helen, holding fast to Laodice's hand, came behind me. We climbed the steps to the open terrace above the Scaean Gate, which looks out over the great sloping plain to where the straits called the Hellespont meet the Aegean Sea.

My father had already arrived; my mother stood hanging on to his arm. People were filing in behind them, searching the horizon.

Greek ships covered the silver sea, rounding the island of Tenedos like a river of dragonflies, a thousand painted galleys in blues and reds and oranges, their square sails taut in the wind.

Men glanced over at Hector as if waiting to hear their first battle orders. But my brother said nothing. None of the children cried out. We stood like statues, surrounded by the whoosh of the wind, and still they kept coming, those proud-masted ships, rounding the westernmost point of the island and scudding toward Troy.

Paris came up behind Helen and wrapped his arms around her. "Have no fear," I heard him whisper. "Aphrodite has promised you to me. The goddess will protect us." He bent to kiss her neck, and her body went limp against him.

Helenus silently urged his brother to keep a proper distance. Kissing in public is frowned upon, though Paris always laughed at such prohibitions. And their passion was so burning, so intimate, that Paris and Helen didn't need to touch to make onlookers uncomfortable. We all felt embarrassed in their presence, as if we had just entered their private bedchamber.

This was the worst possible time for a display of passion. My brother Paris, who thought only of his own pleasure, would never have noticed. But the Trojan women gathered on that terrace would gladly have thrown Helen from the walls if their men had allowed it.

I glared over at her and shook my head. Shamefaced, she pulled away from him.

CHAPTER SEVEN

❧

There's an old saying: "The gods test those they love." We Trojan women who looked down on those ships must have been well loved. The six years that followed brought us tests even Helenus could not have predicted.

That terrace above the Scaean Gate became an auditorium from which we watched the battles. At first light the Greeks marched up from their camp in silence, shoulder to shoulder, raising a cloud of dust. Our warriors were not so reserved. They sounded like a huge flock of birds as they poured forth from our gates, with catcalls to the Greeks and shouts of encouragement to one another.

Noblemen in chariots followed after the foot soldiers. Whenever they saw an enemy warrior cut off from his men, they swooped down and attacked with their long spears. For those of us who watched from the walls, it seemed chaotic, as warriors clashed with spears and swords, shot arrows, or threw large rocks at one another.

During the first weeks Helen was caught up in the excitement. She stayed beside my father, pointing out champions who had been her suitors: Mighty Ajax, son of Telamon, holding his great shield like a tower; Lesser Ajax of Locris, who could outrun the deer; gray-bearded Idomeneus, whose accuracy with the spear was legendary.

One Greek warrior we recognized without Helen's help. We knew Achilles by his long golden hair. Greek noblemen cut their locks at the outset of manhood, but Achilles had left home to join Agamemnon's army before his time for the hair cutting ritual. Although he fought with the strength of ten men, he kept this symbol of boyhood. But more than this, we soon learned to identify Achilles by the dance of death he performed around his intended victim. Our maidens were half in love with him, even as they watched him slice off the straps of their brothers' breastplates in preparation for the final sword thrust. There was something terrible about the way he loved the killing. I tried not to look at him, down on the field, but would find myself drawn to his place of slaughter in spite of myself.

I watched as he sent many of our finest warriors to the Land of the Dead. In time we came to measure those years according to the princes we lost. My sad-faced suitor Coroebus was one of his first victims. My brother Pandarus fell under his sword during another year of the fighting. There were many, many more who left this life in the prime of manhood, deaths too numerous for our bards to sing of.

In the summer of the third year my suitor Othronus died within sight of the gate. A spear drove through his metal corselet and into his stomach. Othronus rolled out of his chariot, dead on the spot, and the horses he had so skillfully commanded reared in panic and galloped off.

I had seen Othronus only on rare occasions during those years, and no marriage arrangement had ever been made. Still, I volunteered to wash the blood and dirt from his body before it was placed upon the pyre. Helen stayed beside me, rinsing the rags in clean water each time I handed one to her.

"How beautiful he is," she said tearfully, patting my shoulder.

I know what she was thinking—that I would never have this beautiful male in my bed. "I never wanted him as a husband," I insisted.

"Then what are you crying for?"

"I'm not crying!"

"There are tears in your eyes!"

I sighed. "He didn't even have the honor of being killed by Achilles."

She eyed me critically.

"I'm wishing he had never heard of Troy, that he'd lived a long, happy life training his Thracian ponies and producing a dozen blond children with a wife as simple and devoted as Andromache."

"Are you so sure?" she asked softly.

"If you really want to help, you'll stop feeling sorry for me and get some more almond oil," I snapped, not knowing what I felt.

She took the jar from my hands. "Hector will avenge his death," she said, still trying to comfort me.

I nodded sadly. That's what this was all about, after all, killing and avenging. They had Achilles, we had Hector, my kind, honorable brother. The Greeks called him Manslaughtering Hector. Other brothers had distinguished themselves in the fighting as well. Helenus was our finest archer. Deiphobus was absolutely fearless, delivering death to hundreds of Greeks with his well-aimed spear. Even Paris, who usually didn't make it down to the field before noon, fought bravely once he got there, a leopard skin slung over his shoulder, although he avoided one-on-one conflicts with the Greek heroes.

But in spite of the ardor of champions on both sides, every battle ended in stalemate. At sunset our forces could always retreat to the safety of our great, circular walls, which the Greeks were unable to scale, just as the legends had predicted. And the Greeks returned to their tents to gaze out at the great sea that separated them from their wives and families.

Soon after Othronus's death Greek contingents began sailing up the Hellespont to raid the cities of our Thracian allies, which stood unprotected. Achilles led his battalion of Myrmidons to Andromache's home kingdom, Thebes, where they slaughtered her father, King Eetion, and all seven of her brothers.

In the women's quarters we mourned our losses and prayed for our enemy to sail away for good. But even in this time of war our days followed their rhythms. Babies were born, barley ground into meal, grapes danced into wine, flax spun and woven into cloth. Helen completed a great wall hanging of purple wool into which she embroidered pictures of the battles fought in her name.

During the early years our Lycian allies were able to supply fresh meat. Lemons and oranges grew within our walls, as well as grapes for wine and enough root vegetables to feed our people. Anticipating a long siege, we had set aside corn and barley in vast storehouses attached to the inner walls. Shoppers at the open market—all the while cursing Helen and especially Paris for bringing these troubles down upon us—could still buy chickens and onions and wine.

Then, in the first month of the sixth year, Andromache gave birth to a live son. They named him Astyanax, and he brought good fortune. Breaks in the fighting grew longer; it sometimes seemed that the Greeks had forgotten about us. I never understood why our army didn't wipe out the stragglers that remained in our harbor. Perhaps Hector knew the real threat to our city was Achilles, who would eventually have to be dealt with on his return.

When spring came with its wild flowers, it was often safe to climb up into the foothills behind our city walls. We women would take the laundry to a hidden valley, where we bathed in snow-fed pools and splashed one another with water as much as we scrubbed tunics.

I remember a particular outing the week of Polyxena's nineteenth birthday. Andromache, whose presence always put a damper on my enjoyment, had decided not to come with us. The hills were carpeted with wild anemones, in blues and whites, the sunlight so intoxicating I felt as if I could bound up the mountainside in a single stride.

Carrying baskets of dirty linens, singing our songs, my sisters and I, with Helen and her three ladies, followed the path to our favorite pool, which was deeper than we had ever seen it. We scrubbed the clothes with pumice sand and spread them on flat rocks to dry, then stripped down to our slips and stepped into the water. It came up to our shoulders, cool under the warm sun. Sunshine glistened on the ripples; the fine, sandy bottom caressed our bare feet.

After a picnic of bread, goat cheese, figs, and wine, I spread a blanket in the shade of a laurel tree and drifted in and out of sleep as I listened to Laodice chatter with Clymene, one of Helen's maids, about a handsome young prince name Helicaon. Laodice was sure the boy had taken an interest in her. Knowing Laodice, it was more likely the other way around, and the boy didn't have a chance.

Helen sat cross-legged, playing her flute and smiling to herself as she listened to Laodice's story. Polyxena, still knee-deep at the edge of the pool, was singing the words to a love song Helen had taught us: "Aphrodite, bless my heart with the joy of love. . . ."

At nineteen Polyxena had become a beautiful woman, with a mass of reddish hair, fair skin, and our father's slightly slanted blue eyes. She swayed back and forth as she sang Helen's love song. Her slip clung to her young breasts. I wondered what chances for love she would have, with this war devouring our noblemen faster than we could produce them. She was such a timid soul. She never complained, never spoke of marriage. Did she feel cheated of the courtship and betrothal gifts?

Much more outgoing than her sister, twelve-year-old Laodice had begun to follow young Helicaon with her eyes whenever he rode forth from the gates, as if praying he would return safely. Theirs would be an excellent match, and I liked the fact that Laodice seemed to have chosen him herself. But would the boy survive long enough to be married? And would Father be willing to arrange matches for his daughters so long as this endless war dragged on?

I didn't want to think about what would happen to me if he did. I had not changed my feelings about marriage. I shut my eyes and willed myself back into the pleasant half sleep I'd been enjoying.

Above our heads some startled sparrows chattered. I propped myself on an elbow and looked around. Helen had put down her flute and was staring up at a high rock that dominated the glen.

There, like a bronze statue silhouetted in the sun, stood Achilles, our enemy. Polyxena, still singing in her pure, rich voice, didn't know he was there watching her. Laodice had jumped to her feet, and I did the same, ready to throw myself in front of my sister's body and at the same instant knowing how useless that would be.

Achilles addressed Helen as if they had just met in polite company. "My lady, Queen Helen, who is this young noble-woman?"

"She is Polyxena, daughter of King Priam," Helen replied.

"And you are not allowed to speak to us! Or to hunt in these mountains!" said Laodice, her hands on her hips.

Achilles made a mock bow to my brave little sister. "Accept my apologies." He glanced back at Polyxena, who had turned toward him, her face flushed. "I thought I had come upon a goddess, or a wood nymph bathing in the pool." He smiled at her, a very private smile, and then disappeared into the trees.

There was a moment of stunned silence, then Helen rushed to my side. "Did you see how he looked at her?" she asked excitedly.

I stood and folded the blanket, willing myself not to be angry.

"Without Achilles, the Greeks would stop fighting. They'd

have to! Cassandra, listen to me, maybe we could arrange a match between them!"

"You forget; this is the man who has butchered our brothers and cousins." I shook my head. How could Helen understand? She was a Greek, after all. This was her kinsman, and an honored kinsman at that. "Clymene, see that they pick up all the laundry! We're going home. Polyxena, put your robe on!"

But my sister didn't hear me. Polyxena was staring up at the rock with the same startled expression, that of the hare the instant before the fox pounces, fascinated by the certainty of its own death.

CHAPTER EIGHT

༺꧂

Achilles must have been part of a general advance. In the next week all the Greek contingents came back to base camp. Their three years of raiding had amassed considerable booty, distributed among them according to rank and individual accomplishment. But despite these profits, we heard from our spies that the Greeks had grown tired of foreign adventures. Their ships' timbers needed repairs, their rigging was loose. They wanted to finish this six-year war and go home to their wives and children. They attacked now in earnest.

We saw a month of the fiercest fighting so far, the most terrible losses. Antenor, our chief minister, gave a speech in the council urging Helen's return to her lawful husband. Helen was afraid to leave her rooms, and people gave Paris the evil eye wherever he went.

Then a miracle happened. We heard about it from a wine merchant who had been supplying the Greeks while spying for us. He came immediately with the news, which he knew would earn him a nugget of gold. "Down in the Greek camp," he told Father, "your two most powerful enemies have started their own private war."

Father nodded slowly. "Agamemnon and . . . the other has to be Achilles."

"The very two, and fighting over the distribution of prizes. Achilles had him a dusky girl named Briseis, took her from her father in a raid on the southern islands. Agamemnon demanded her for himself. Just to rile the boy is my opinion. The two have hated each other from the start."

"Get to the point, man. What has fighting over slave girls to do with war?"

"Achilles called Agamemnon 'dog face,' told him he'd made a botch of the whole campaign. Would have pulled out his sword if Odysseus hadn't stopped him! In the end the young prince had to give the girl over. But he's refusing to fight."

My father sat smiling, rubbing his beard.

"Says he never had a quarrel with the Trojans in the first place."

Father said, "Achilles was too young to have sworn the Oath of the Horse. He had no obligation to avenge Menelaus."

"That's just what the boy is saying, my lord. And they'll never take Troy without him."

Father called it a sign from Zeus that our fortunes had turned, once and for all. At the Greek camp Achilles sat sulking outside his tent. His beloved cousin Patroclus, a musician and skilled healer, played the lyre to console him. Meanwhile, Odysseus and the other kings struggled to mediate the quarrel. They would all have given their own concubines—and thrown in some wives and daughters—to see Achilles lead his dreaded Myrmidon troops once more into battle.

But Achilles would make no deals. He remained idle, staring out at the blue-green Aegean, nursing his rage. His men amused themselves with javelin and archery contests and wandered aimlessly around the camp. Their horses stood chomping clover and marsh grass, growing fat.

These were days of glory for Troy. The Greeks still outnumbered us, but without Achilles their men lost heart. At one point a handful of infantrymen began a full-scale retreat to the ships. Only Odysseus's eloquence kept them from sailing home and leaving their noble leaders to fight on alone.

Father made a speech in the council about our salvaged pride and sacrificed an unblemished white bull with gilded horns to Zeus, The Great Cloudgatherer, our protector. Hector's face glowed with pride. Even Andromache seemed to relax.

That evening Helen dared visit me once more in the women's quarters. She was wearing a red robe; she had braided silver ropes into her hair. Flushed with excitement, she announced, "I have a plan."

I was cross-legged on the floor sorting wool from one of the trinket boxes. I glanced up, still twisting blue strands around my index finger. "Does this plan have anything to do with Polyxena?"

"Just hear me out—and try not to get angry." She sat down beside me, hugging her knees. "Achilles has deserted the Greek cause," she began tentatively.

"I know."

"Well, you saw how he looked at Polyxena."

I shivered, remembering that look. "Father would never hear of it."

"Don't be too sure. Especially if Polyxena were willing . . ."

"*Willing?* Did you see the way she looked at *him!*"

Helen smiled. "There was a fascination in that fear," she said, reaching for a puff of violet wool.

I had pulled my thread until the tip of my finger was white, but I remained silent.

"I'll talk to her," she said. "Helenus could act as go-between. He's well respected on both sides."

My heart had begun to pound inside my rib cage.

"Just one word from you . . ."

"Never!" I shouted. "You'd sacrifice my sister to save yourself!"

"To save Troy!" she cried, and then, "Andromache said you wouldn't listen."

"*Andromache?* You two have no right to speak of marriages! You're both outsiders to our family!"

I felt a pang of unnamed fear as she replaced the purple wool and got up. "You don't speak for the women of your family," she said.

I went after her then, knocking over the trinket box as I scrambled to my feet. I grabbed her arm, my fingers digging into her pale skin. "You'll go no further with this!"

She twisted away, eyes frightened.

"Promise me," I hissed.

"Cassandra, you're hurting me!"

And while Helen and I struggled in the women's quarters, another kind of struggle was taking place down below in the men's hall. Our brother Deiphobus was convincing Paris to challenge Menelaus in single combat.

CHAPTER NINE

꧁꧂

B uilt like an acrobat and much quicker on his feet, Paris had so far managed to keep out of Menelaus's grasp. Each time my brother slipped away from Helen's stocky, bowlegged husband on the battlefield, the Greeks shouted insults. But while Paris laughed off these assaults to his manhood, they wounded our brother Deiphobus to the core. For all the years of the war Deiphobus had been trying to make Paris stand and fight. On this night of celebration in the men's hall he finally succeeded.

Paris was, as usual, making light of the accusations of cowardice. "They're right! I *am* a curly-headed wife snatcher," he told his brothers.

Hector shook his head wearily. Deiphobus sat frowning into his wine.

"But I did not choose these fine features or this golden hair. After all," Paris said, nudging Deiphobus, "who can deny the gods' gifts? Could Helenus here have refused his thick lashes and soulful brown eyes? Could Hector have refused his integrity?"

"I dare you to step forward and challenge Menelaus," Deiphobus interrupted.

Paris shrugged and then downed his wine. No one spoke.

For Deiphobus, pride was everything. All his life he had mimicked the actions of our eldest brother, while lacking Hector's noble heart. Now he refilled Paris's gold cup and added, "I'll bet you don't want to give Helen the chance to measure you against him."

Paris was very drunk. He had been playing draughts all night and was already deeply in debt to Deiphobus. "Name your bet," he said.

"I'll wager against your most precious possession."

Paris looked up, eyes narrowed.

"Helen. She's mine if you don't find the courage."

"This is madness," Helenus said. "Menelaus has dreamed of killing you ever since he returned to Sparta and found an empty bed. He hates you more than you could ever know."

Deiphobus pushed him aside. "Don't you want to find out what sort of a man it is whose wife you have been keeping?"

Paris's grip tightened on his wine cup. For once he had no joking answer.

"How does Helen feel when your own people see you as a public pest?" Deiphobus pressed. "When her kinsmen guffaw at the sight of you?"

Just after dawn Helenus shook me awake with the news that Paris planned to challenge the Greeks to send forth a champion to fight him. Of course we knew who would answer that call.

"He'll never go through with it," I said. "Paris is good with the javelin and the bow. But man to man? Menelaus will tear him apart."

"Just in case, send Laodice to fetch Helen. Have them meet you atop the Scaean Gate. Paris is downstairs arming himself, and I must do the same." My brother paused before going out the door. "Poor soul, that she should have to see this contest played out."

I was beyond feeling sorry for Helen. I had let her go the night before without having made her promise to abandon her matchmaking. Now I regretted my softness. Still, I woke Laodice, told her the news, and sent her off to Helen's rooms.

The two of them arrived on the gate in time to see Paris step out of the Trojan ranks, his leopard skin slung over his shoulder. He shook his two spears and challenged all comers to fight him. While the Greeks buzzed among themselves, he strode about in the open space between the two armies. Every few seconds he glanced up at Helen, who stood clutching the edge of the parapet, her pale hair uncombed and blowing in her face. Then we saw the Greek flanks parting to allow a chariot to pass through—Menelaus's chariot.

"Immortal gods!" cried Helen. "*Menelaus* has seen him!"

As soon as Paris saw his challenger, he retreated inside the Trojan ranks. Hector caught hold of him, speaking earnestly into his ear while the Greeks jeered and Menelaus shouted, "There will be little left of your blond hair and good looks when I get through with you!"

Helen said, "I wish I had died before I followed your brother here. . . ."

"Look!" Laodice said. "Hector's bringing him back!"

Hector had a hand on Paris's shoulder, guiding him back toward the Greek lines, where he proclaimed his brother ready to fight Menelaus for Helen and all her wealth.

Both armies cheered loudly. Trojans and Greeks took off their armor and sat down facing each other. My father was called down to the field to swear the agreement, with Agamemnon representing the Greek coalition. The two poured a libation to honor Zeus, then measured out a space for the duel. They put clay shards into a helmet and shook them. The two warriors drew for first spear cast.

Paris won. We watched him bind his calves with silver-trimmed greaves, which protected his legs from ankle to knee, and put on his bronze helmet with a lofty horsehair plume. Helen glanced over at me, eyes brimming with tears, but I refused to meet her eyes. We were joined by Polyxena, holding little Astyanax, and then Andromache, my mother, and four of her ladies. All had heard the news in the women's quarters.

Menelaus was first to step into the measured space. One of Mother's ladies whispered that he was built like a prize bull.

From the Trojan side entered Paris. "Ah! Handsome as Apollo," another cried out.

The armies fell silent as the two warriors began circling to the right. Both had learned as boys in the gymnasium this movement that gives the right-handed warrior a natural advantage. With shield strapped across the left forearm to ward off attack and spear poised behind the right shoulder, the right arm would exert maximum thrust when the time came.

Gradually, the circles tightened, and twice Menelaus shouted insults, hoping to anger Paris. Menelaus, the seasoned veteran, no doubt knew such emotion would cause a lapse in concentration. But Paris ignored the taunts and kept circling; his eyes blazed at his enemy, moving ever to the right.

For the two combatants now facing each other, all the years of their lives had funneled into this time and space. On this summer morning, in a clearing on the windy plains of Troy, one of them would die. The other would take home the world's most beautiful woman and all her treasure.

I didn't know what I wanted to see happen. Of course I wanted the war to end. But if Menelaus took Helen away, there would be an emptiness in Troy. We had accumulated six years of memories, Helen and I—of teaching each other our languages and laughing at the mistakes, of sharing patterns at the loom and playing knucklebones with Laodice and Polyxena during the long afternoons. I still found such women's games pointless. But I loved to listen to Helen's stories, to hear her laughter. Even as angry as I was, I knew how I would miss her.

Down on the field the pace had quickened. Paris lunged forward, menacing Menelaus with a spear, then leaping back. As this dance of death reached its climax, each warrior must have perceived his opponent not as a man with a name and face but as a dark moving shape. Toward the end of the final circle of feinting and parrying Menelaus lowered his left arm, exposing his chest, and Paris hurled his spear.

His throw was true, but Menelaus had expected it. Like

the insults, the dropping of his shield had been a ploy. In the spear's split-second trajectory Menelaus lifted his shield to intercept it and then, in one continuous motion, hurled his own spear against the round target of Paris's shield.

I heard my mother draw in her breath. The spear drove through six layers of hide and bronze. Paris swerved to one side, twisting his torso to avoid the point as the momentum knocked him to the ground.

This chain of events was clear only afterward. At the time we thought Paris had been wounded, perhaps fatally. During those long seconds of waiting Helen was rigid with terror. Polyxena, still holding the baby, moved closer to her side.

Struggling to get up, Paris dropped his shield, and we saw the spear embedded in it, but no blood on his chest. Mother let out a sigh of relief.

Then Menelaus drew his sword and brought it down on Paris's helmet. The blade broke into pieces. Bellowing in rage, Menelaus grabbed the helmet's horsehair crest and dragged Paris back toward the Greek ranks. My brother's body was limp, unresisting.

"The strap is choking him!" Laodice cried.

"I cannot watch!" Helen hid her face against Polyxena's shoulder as the baby gurgled and reached out to grab her golden hair.

None of us breathed—even Andromache, who would most gladly have seen our brother strangled—until the helmet came off in Menelaus's hand.

"The helmet strap! It's snapped!" Laodice said to Helen. "Menelaus is tossing the helmet over his shoulder."

Paris scrambled to his knees just as one of the Greeks passed Menelaus a spear to finish him off. Helen heard us gasp.

"Has Menelaus killed him?" she breathed.

"No, wait! We can't see what's happening."

A ground-level swirl of dust had appeared from nowhere, enveloping both warriors.

"Cassandra, what is it?"

I shook my head, mystified. There hadn't been a cloud in the sky. Now the open space between the two armies was covered in a blanket of gray. When it burned off moments later, Paris had disappeared.

"You can open your eyes," I said to Helen. "He's gone."

"Trojan treachery!" Menelaus bellowed. "Where are you hiding him?" But Hector and Deiphobus looked as bewildered as any of the Greeks.

Greek and Trojan noblemen wandered in the measured space, studying the parched earth. Menelaus was running back and forth like a wild beast, shouting, *"Traitors!* Where are you hiding him?"

Andromache turned to Helen then. Only my mother's presence kept her from speaking the truth: that there was no one among our kinsmen who would have hidden Paris from his death. "They should look for him back in his lady's bedchamber," Andromache said, glaring at Helen. "That's his place of preference, while his brothers are down on the plains fighting his battles. Perhaps *you* can find him and persuade him to return to this quarrel that he himself began?"

Color drained from Helen's face. "Cassandra, come with me," she said.

I shook my head.

"Please!"

"You weren't afraid to be alone with him when he was a guest at your husband's table," Andromache said.

Helen looked from Andromache to me, her hair blowing in the wind, her shoulders heaving with silent sobs. Then she turned and ran.

I followed, angry at my own weakness.

CHAPTER TEN

❧

P aris was stretched out on their bed, his hair wet
from a bath he had just taken to wash away the
grime of battle.

"Andromache was right!" Helen cried. "Oh, what will
she think of us?"

"Come here, my love," he said, patting the place next to
him. "Welcome me back from the edge of death."

But she stayed in the center of the room. "I wish you *had*
died! I wish Menelaus had killed you! What will your
brothers think?" She darted a glance at where I stood in the
open doorway. "What will the women say?"

Paris adjusted the cloth around his waist and then leaned
back against the silk cushions, arms crossed behind his head.
"Don't scold me. Scold the gods. Menelaus has triumphed
because Athena helped him. But I have supporters too.
Aphrodite sent that cloud to cover my escape, surrounded as
I was by the enemy, one man against a multitude."

"Your contest was with Menelaus alone," I said from the
doorway. "None of the others would have touched you."

"Enough talk of battle. Can we never escape it?"

"My sister Cassandra," he said to Helen, "is one of my severest critics. Did she tell you she was first to recognize me when I came back to Troy to compete in the Annual Games? Instead of welcoming me to the family, she told Father to send me back to the mountains. But she loves *you*, my dear. And Cassandra will fight like a tigress to protect the few people she loves. She'll leave us alone if you ask her nicely."

Helen's face wore the same battered expression it had the night before, when she ran from me in the women's quarters.

Paris said to her, "I never wanted you more, even when I carried you off in my ship and we spent the night on that island. Come, don't be coy. Cassandra understands these things."

Helen begged me with sad blue eyes to forgive her weakness. And what a weakness love is! I was sure she found Menelaus the better man. But it didn't matter that the Greeks made jokes about Paris, that his own people despised him. The sound of his voice was like honey to her ears; she would follow him anywhere.

Without a word of reproach I closed the door behind me. No wonder people called it Aphrodite's madness. I prayed to all the gods I would never fall victim to it.

As I made my way back to the walls, I was finding it difficult to remain angry. Helen couldn't help plotting to stay in Troy, with him, no matter what—or whom—she had to sacrifice. Even my sister. I realized I had overreacted to her plans. Helen had no real backing in our family. Except for Laodice and Polyxena, the women shuddered with hatred at the sight of her. Especially Andromache. It was foolish to think the two might conspire to marry off Polyxena.

Back atop the Scaean Gate my sister Laodice stood beside my mother, watching the renewed fighting. Andromache and Polyxena had gone home with the baby. I nodded at my mother's questioning look. "He's all right. I just left him in his rooms. With Helen."

"Hector will need to know," she said, sighing.

Before I could call for a messenger, Laodice pulled me to the wall to report what had happened in the time I'd been away.

"Who broke the truce?" I asked, looking down at the scramble of bodies, the panic-stricken horses, the dust and the blood.

"Right after you left, Menelaus announced his victory and all the Greeks cheered. He shouted at Father that it was Hector's *duty* to hand over Helen. . . ."

"Hector would like nothing better," my mother murmured. "But your father will never agree."

The field was littered with flyspecked corpses, men who had once been fathers and husbands and brothers. A duel was taking place directly below us. I watched Agamemnon plunge his spear into the chest of a Trojan warrior who fell over backward, vomiting blood. I watched Agamemnon set his foot on his victim's chest and draw out his spear. Shouts of victory and screams of terror pounded in my ears. The pointlessness of this dying—and my own helplessness to stop it—washed over me, as it had so many times before.

"Menelaus said we were hiding Paris. That we had trampled our oath underfoot. Cassandra, listen!" Laodice had to pull my sleeve to get my attention. "And then someone— one of our men—shot an arrow at Menelaus! Blood was running down his legs—like the scarlet dye on ivory cheek pieces for horses—and he was still standing and shaking his fist at us! Their surgeon carried him off the field and the two sides rushed at each other."

"Which Trojan broke the truce?"

"None did," Mother said. "It was the goddess's doing. Athena disguised herself and came down among our archers. It was she who shot that arrow. We all know she intends to make a wilderness of our city."

"Mother says Athena doesn't *want* us to make peace," Laodice added. "Do you think it's true about the golden apple? That Hera and Athena hate us because Paris awarded it to Aphrodite?"

"Who can tell what's true and what Paris invents? He's saying that Aphrodite sent that cloud—to allow him to get away from Menelaus."

"What other explanation can there be?" Mother interrupted. She adjusted her veil around a crown of silver braids, her handsome face controlled but her hands unsteady. I regretted my words. People were accusing her of having bribed the shepherd who'd been charged with disposing of Paris on the mountainside. Clearly, she still loved this son who had brought us seven years of war. In fact, Paris was probably her second favorite son, next to Hector. But if the stories were true, did she ever feel responsible for having saved his life? Is that why she blamed all our present troubles on the gods?

"What can we do when immortals descend from Olympus and take sides?" she said, as if reading my mind.

I asked myself for the thousandth time which side had the most powerful backers. This was a question debated endlessly in the women's quarters, in the market, in stables, kitchens, and slaves' huts. Aphrodite seemed to have aligned herself with Paris; Athena fought for her Greeks. People were less sure of Zeus's intentions, and he outranked all the others.

Mother was still talking about the latest heavenly interventions when Laodice spotted Hector down on the field, making his way back toward the gate. By the time he came through, a dozen women had gathered under the oak tree just inside and were begging news of their husbands and sons.

We followed Mother down three flights of stairs to rescue him. Shooing the women away, the queen took her son by the hand. "Let me bring you some wine," she said. "You can pour a libation to Father Zeus and have a drink yourself."

"No wine for me, Mother. And I can't offer prayers to Zeus bespattered with blood." He set down his spear but didn't bother to remove his helmet, although sweat ran down his forehead. The blood of Greek warriors had dried in rivulets on his muscular forearms.

"I came to ask *you* to approach Athena, since she appears to hate us so," he said. "Gather the older women and go to her temple. Tell her we'll sacrifice twelve unblemished heifers if only she'll have pity on the wives and children of Troy."

Mother left immediately to summon the women, probably relieved to have something to do. Smiling wearily, Hector sat down on a stone bench and reached out a hand to Laodice, who sat beside him and leaned her head against his shoulder.

"We've missed you so," she told him. "Andromache and

Astyanax were here just a moment ago. Astyanax has a new tooth."

"Don't send for my wife," he said to me. "Spare her the sight of me like this." He wiped sweat from his eyes. "Cassandra, have you seen Helen? She'll know what happened to Paris. . . ."

"She's with him. In his chambers—Wait! Rest a moment—I'll go get him."

Hector shook off my restraining hand. "How can he hide while men are dying for his sake!"

"He says it was Aphrodite's doing. That the goddess sent the cloud to cover his retreat. Dear brother, let me get him for you. Laodice will order goat cheese and wine while you wait."

"No, Cassandra. He'll have to answer to *me*!" Hector shook his head then and laughed. "The Greeks are accusing *us* of hiding him. By Zeus Thunderer, if our allies knew, they would sail away at once."

And if Menelaus knew where Paris was at this moment, I thought to myself, he would storm our great walls single-handedly. But I didn't want to tell Hector that Paris was in bed with Helen, that he'd just taken a cool bath. Hector hadn't slept with his own wife but once in the past month. He'd been taking his few hours of sleep in a temporary camp outside the walls.

Andromache's arrival provided the delay I needed. She came running to meet her husband. The nurse followed, carrying their happy, cherub-faced baby, and for a moment Hector forgot about his brother. He stood smiling down at the boy, his eyes filling with tears. Andromache wept openly. She stood on tiptoes and threw her arms around Hector.

"Your father says you'll ask the Greeks to send forth a champion to meet you in single combat. Pity me and stay behind the walls."

Hector stroked her glossy black hair. "Don't worry, love. I've learned to handle myself in battle. My only fear is for you and for my son. That's what keeps me fighting."

He held out his hands to Astyanax, but the child was frightened by the tossing horsehair plume on his father's helmet and clung to the nurse. Smiling, my brother removed his helmet and set it down on the bench. Andromache laughed through her tears as Hector cradled Astyanax and then held him up above his head while the boy shrieked with glee.

I slipped away while they laughed together and hurried through the deserted streets. At Paris's apartment I found Clymene, Helen's maid, in the courtyard. "Tell Paris Hector is on his way," I told her. "Pound on the door until he answers you."

CHAPTER ELEVEN

∼◦∼

When Hector arrived, he found his younger brother in Helen's outer chamber, where the looms were kept. Paris sat fingering his bow. His silver-trimmed corselet lay on the floor where he had dropped it after his miraculous rescue.

"Don't *you* scold me," Paris said, looking up at Hector, who was visibly working to master his anger. "Helen is calling me unstable and Cassandra here shows me no mercy, as usual. Says I'm a disgrace to the family."

"You *are* a disgrace to the family," I said.

Paris dismissed me with a wave of the hand. "Just wait while I put on my armor," he said to Hector. "I'll tell you the story of my escape on the way to the gate."

Perhaps wanting to redeem himself in Helen's eyes, Paris armed himself and hurried off with his brother, loping down the path like a stallion after a fresh feed.

Back on the field he handled his bow brilliantly, sending well-armed arrows of death to a score of Greeks. But he had no plans to complete his duel with Menelaus, or even to allow Menelaus, who had come limping back to battle, anywhere near him.

The Greeks redoubled their insults, calling him "handsome coward" and "barbarian seducer." That night at the council Antenor again proposed the return of Helen.

"We have broken our truce," the white-haired nobleman said, frowning over at Paris. "The gods won't approve of such faithlessness."

This time there was a loud chorus of agreement. Paris had to shout to be heard. "I *will not* give up my woman! But wait! Hear me out! All the wealth I brought with her from Sparta I will agree to return."

The grumbling subsided.

"And I'll give Menelaus two bronze tripods from Sidon. A silver girdle with lapis inlay."

This offer was immediately conveyed to the Greek camp. Two hours later they sent their herald refusing it. Hector dispatched the herald with a challenge for a champion of their own choosing to meet him in single combat.

I heard news of these events the following day in Helenus's apartment. I had found my twin in his rooms, to which he'd retreated after a full night and all morning spent in emergency meetings.

"I suppose Father is praying Menelaus will accept," I said to my twin, "so that Hector can finish what Paris began."

When Helenus ignored me and continued to pace the floor, I asked, "That would reinstate our family pride, wouldn't it?"

Helenus snorted in frustration. "*What* family pride? What do we have to be proud of? Deiphobus is insisting Helen be given over to him, threatening to take her himself. Meanwhile, Paris says he's lived up to *their* agreement. He challenged Menelaus. The wager did not stipulate winning—

or staying around to be killed, as Paris puts it. We're reduced to brawling among ourselves. Our own nobles are laughing at us. A company of Thracians has already pulled out, set sail for home."

"Sit down and eat something," I interrupted.

"Eat? We haven't had meat on our tables in over a month. If we slaughter the last of the goats, there'll be no more cheese. We'll run out of grain by the end of summer. . . . Besides"—Helenus stopped pacing and looked down at me—"Agamemnon will never allow his younger brother to stand against Hector. Even if Menelaus weren't wounded, Hector's by far the better man."

"Andromache is afraid Achilles will step forward."

"Not likely." Helenus resumed his pacing. "It has to be Ajax. He's the best they've got with Achilles out of it. Can Hector take him? That's the real question."

"You're exhausted. They depend too much on your good judgement." I poured a cup of wine and put it into his hand, closing his fingers around the stem. "Come, sit down."

He lowered himself onto the couch and sipped distractedly, then leaned back against the wall, closing his eyes. "Where will it end?" he said softly.

I shook my head. That was a question I asked myself a hundred times each day.

I left my brother after he'd eaten the figs and bread I'd brought and drunk the honeyed wine, into which I'd dissolved some sleeping powder. Our nobles counted on Helenus to keep them from each other's throats, I thought as I passed through the corridor that connected the rooms of Priam's sons with the stairway to the main courtyard. The strain on him was beginning to show.

And beyond the battles and the diplomacy I knew my brother was haunted by visions of the future. During sleepless nights he agonized over the food shortages the siege had begun to produce, the scarcity of medicines and firewood and replacement parts for chariots.

Passing a window, I happened to glance down into the kitchen garden. Seated together on a stone bench were Helen and Andromache. At first I was struck by this unlikely combination. Andromache hated to be in the same room as Helen. Instinctively, I pulled back to avoid being seen. I was too far away to hear their words, only the hushed, confidential voices. I ran to the end of the corridor and, taking off my sandals, tiptoed to the bottom of the staircase, where I could hide just inside the doorway.

"Cassandra will fight. . . ." Helen was saying, and then, "You were right. . . ." I still couldn't catch all the words.

Next came Andromache's louder, more lilting, northern intonation. "Cassandra does not make these decisions. Priam would open dowry negotiations."

"Can we count on his support?"

I forced myself to remain quiet.

"You know what a proud man he is. Imagine having the most glorious warrior of all time as a son-in-law."

"Achilles has behaved honorably . . . taken pity on younger warriors . . . ransomed them to their fathers."

"Let's not forget the queen. She has reason enough for approving this marriage . . . to preserve the sons that still survive," Andromache added, always mindful of Hector's safety.

"What about Polyxena's safety?" I cried out, stepping forth from the doorway. Helen's face registered fear, then shame. *"How could you?"* I shouted at her.

Andromache got up and stood between us. "Civilized people have always used marriage to cement alliances. To prevent bloodshed," she said in a matter-of-fact tone.

"What other weapons do we have to protect our loved ones?" Helen cried. "Would you have us put on armor and rush down to the field, like Amazons?"

"Yes!"

Helen was weeping. Andromache stayed between us, arms crossed. "You've always lived in a dream world," she said to me. "Polyxena was raised to marry a great warrior. What finer destiny than to bear Achilles' legitimate children?"

"He's born of the immortals!" Helen murmured.

"Haven't you watched him on the field?" I cried. "Seen how much he loves the killing?"

Andromache shook her head impatiently. "I don't pretend to understand such things."

"Has anyone asked *her* if she wants to bear his children?"

But I never got my answer. Andromache's servant came running with news. The Greeks were sending Ajax to meet Hector. Hector had gone to arm himself, and our people were already lining the walls, fighting for the better vantage points, so that they could tell the story of this duel to their grandchildren.

CHAPTER TWELVE

❧

The two warriors were perfectly matched. Both armies sat and marveled at their artistry, forgetting they were at war. A white moon came up in the afternoon sky, and the sun cast lengthening shadows as they threw their spears and swerved to avoid each other's spearpoints in an elegant dance that went on for well over an hour.

Only once in this time did I fear for Hector's safety, when Ajax's spear grazed his neck. Andromache fainted at the blood, but Hector recovered his footing almost instantly and hurled his own spear at his opponent.

I kept looking over at Polyxena, who sat beside our mother on the terrace reserved for the royal family. How innocent she looked, her brow knotted with concern, her reddish brown curls tousled in the wind. At one point I went over and whispered in her ear, "Has Helen spoken to you?"

"About what?" She twisted in her chair and looked up at me as if to say, "Why are you asking such a question when our brother is fighting for his life on the field below?"

My mother was frowning at me. I went back to my own seat. Still, I kept wondering if Polyxena suspected anything. I had no idea how she felt about that brief encounter at the pool, other than her expression of panic when she looked up at Achilles standing above her on the rocks. She had never once spoken of the incident. Polyxena was learning to keep her feelings to herself. In the past months she had become a mystery to me. I wished she were less obedient, more outspoken, like Laodice.

I forced myself to concentrate on the duel, telling myself it was useless to speculate and worry. Besides, Helenus would know what to do.

When the sky turned a deep rose, neither warrior had claimed an advantage, and two heralds, one from each side, came between them, as it was our custom to stop fighting at sunset. Hector said afterward he was relieved he hadn't killed this man he respected so thoroughly. I think Ajax felt the same. As the orange sun dipped into the Aegean, the two exchanged compliments and gifts. Hector gave Ajax his sword; Ajax offered his crimson belt. Both agreed to call the match a draw.

Later that night the Greeks proposed a truce to allow both armies to burn the dead bodies that lay fly-covered and rotting on the rippled plain.

Alone on the walls the next morning I watched their progress. The eerie silence, after the clash of battle, brought an illusion of peace. Enemy warriors occasionally stopped and talked to one another, and it was difficult to tell Greek from Trojan unless you recognized a particular face.

I saw Helenus talking with Odysseus under an olive tree and wondered if the two were reminiscing about the delegation Odysseus once led to Troy, when he gave the clever speech that convinced Father to return Helen to Menelaus.

Neither man had wanted this terrible war. When Agamemnon began collecting his army, Odysseus had refused to join the Greek coalition. He claimed he had no obligation to avenge Menelaus because he had never sworn the Oath of the Horse. Agamemnon had to send King Palamedes to persuade him.

When Palamedes arrived in Ithaca, Odysseus pretended to be crazy. He rushed out to his fields, scattering salt instead of seeds. But Palamedes, who was almost as crafty as Odysseus, grabbed Odysseus's baby and threw him in front of his father's plow. Odysseus, of course, pulled the oxen to a stop, and Palamedes declared he was sane enough to go to war.

That baby son would be nine years old now. Oracles had predicted that Odysseus would need an additional ten years to return home after the war. How desperately he must have been longing to begin that journey!

And my gentle brother Helenus, whose terrible visions invaded his sleep, must have shared this longing as the two watched oxcarts being piled high with bodies. My twin no longer told me of these visions, but I knew they kept him from the boon of sleep. I pitied him this foreknowledge, which I had been spared since the day Helen arrived in our city.

I saw Helenus only briefly that night, on his way to report to the council. "I need to talk to you," I said, falling into step beside him. "Helen and Andromache have been plotting together. . . ."

"Helen and Andromache don't even talk to each other."

"They're talking now." I glanced over my shoulder. "Can we go somewhere alone?"

"I've no time now," he said, studying my face. "I'll come to your rooms in the morning."

But I didn't see him for two days, not until he was brought back to the citadel with a wound for me to mend—and then it was too late to worry about a marriage with Achilles.

CHAPTER THIRTEEN

✦

I n spite of the good feelings generated by the one-
day truce, the Greeks had not lost their thirst for
battle. At first light the following morning they
marched up from their camp, and Trojans poured forth to
meet them with the usual noise and turmoil. Our men were
still outnumbered, but they had just said good-bye to loved
ones. They knew what happened to wives and children
at the hands of a conquering army. Terrified by this
knowledge, they threw themselves at the invaders, fighting
like wild beasts. The tide of battle turned again in Troy's
favor.

We heard stories that Agamemnon would now give
anything—the slave girl Briseis, his own daughters in
marriage—if only Achilles would return to the fight. But
even with his cousin Patroclus begging him to reconsider,
Achilles would not accept his commander's apologies.

Our men penetrated the Greek camp the next afternoon
and set fire to one of their ships. It was after this offensive
that Helenus returned to me with his arm in a sling.
Menelaus's spear had pierced his right hand, pinning it to

the frame of his bow. I washed the wound and sprinkled some bitterroot over the surface to ease the pain.

But Helenus wouldn't sit still and let me care for him. "Patroclus is dead. Hector's killed him," he said, getting up from the chair to pace the floor.

"Sit down," I said. "I need to make a proper bandage."

He obeyed, shaking his head in bewilderment. "Patroclus came marching up from the Greek camp, wearing Achilles' star-studded armor and leading a thousand Myrmidons who had not seen battle in more than a month. He wanted us to think he *was* his invincible cousin. It didn't take us long to recognize him. Still, Patroclus saved their ships and killed a score of Trojans before Hector caught up with him."

"By Zeus Thunderer, hold still and let me work. This is good news, but we've killed Greeks before."

With his free hand Helenus grabbed my arm. "Cassandra, you don't understand. Hector stripped the armor! *Achilles'* armor! Made for him alone by the immortals. Our brother dares wear it into battle!" His eyes were wild. I thought the pain and fever were affecting his reason.

"Don't you *see*?" he cried. "Of all the people on earth Achilles loved his cousin best. Achilles had no real quarrel with Troy before, no reason to hate us. . . ."

And perhaps some reason to love us—or at least one of us, I thought, at first relieved by this turn of events.

"When he returns to the field, he'll show no mercy," Helenus insisted. "He'll be after Hector."

"Has Hector returned the body?"

"He refuses to give it over."

I felt suddenly afraid. The Greeks believe a person's soul

cannot pass over into Hades, the land of the dead, without the proper sacrifices and lamentations at the funeral pyre. Achilles would not be likely to forgive this transgression. Mind you, we Trojans feel just as strongly about the bodies of our own warriors.

"Menelaus straddled the body, like a mountain lion stands over its young," Helenus went on. "Then Ajax came with some lesser warriors. They've made a kind of fence around him with their spears sticking outward. We've surrounded them, raised a great cloud of dust. But those Greeks would rather die than return to Achilles without that body."

Troy had run out of the sacred herbs I needed to treat his wound properly, and there was no way to leave the city to gather them in the mountains. I finally managed to stop the bleeding and apply a dressing. Slaves prepared a bed underneath the gallery, and I sat beside my twin as he drifted in and out of sleep.

Shortly after sunset he groaned, mumbled something about Achilles, clutched my arm, and cried, "Hector, *watch out*! On your left!" He opened his eyes then and released his grip. "Is it night already?" he murmured.

A crescent moon glimmered in a patch of violet sky above the open court. We could hear faint drumming down in the Greek camp.

"They're singing their war chant," I said, and Helenus sang the words softly into the twilight hush:

> *"We will trace rivers of blood around their high walls.*
> *Thick Trojan blood.*
> *Thick barbarian blood. . . ."*

He closed his eyes again and was silent for so long I thought he'd gone back to sleep. "But we barbarians fight harder," he finally said. "We have women and children to protect."

I adjusted the pillows as he struggled to sit up. I winced at the pain on his face when he shifted his arm.

"That's all that keeps me killing down there," he said, "with my feet in red muck. Just like your dream. Remember your dream?"

I nodded and placed another pillow under his arm.

"*You're* what keeps me from setting out across the mountains with a pack of olives and goat cheese," he said. "You, Polyxena, Laodice. Poor faithful Andromache and little Astyanax. Even Helen, who started it all. I wouldn't want her thrown from the walls if her lawful husband won her back."

"Would Menelaus fight this endless war only to murder her?"

"Who knows how he would avenge the wound she inflicted on *him*? Better to keep him at bay. But tell me, you have some news of Helen and Andromache?"

"Never mind about that." I lifted his bandage and examined the fleshy triangle between thumb and index finger. The wound was clean, but would be difficult to heal. I tested his forehead with the back of my hand; his fever had gone down.

"What would prompt Andromache to have anything to do with Helen?"

"Go back to sleep," I said. "It's not a problem anymore." I was frightened by the weariness that was always in his voice lately. I wanted to protect him instead of turning to him for comfort and advice the way I usually did.

CHAPTER FOURTEEN

❧

The next day Achilles raged across the plain like a fire rages across a parched valley. To each new victim he spoke almost lovingly. "My friend, come and die—Why are you crying?—Patroclus had to die, and he was a much better man than you."

A contingent of our panic-stricken infantrymen, confused by the cloud of dust the retreat had kicked up, stampeded into the river to escape his fury. Smiling his thin-lipped smile, Achilles leaned his spear against a tree and leaped in after them. Waist-deep he slashed with his great sword until the water ran red with blood. He spared twelve young noblemen, dragged them out, and after binding them with thongs, sent them back to the Greek camp to be sacrificed at Patroclus's funeral later that night.

We couldn't see these events from our walls. The stories arrived with men straggling back to our city during that endless morning. They reported that the bulk of the army was in a rout, flying before Achilles toward the safety of our citadel.

I was grateful Helenus's wound had kept him inside. My twin stood beside me on top of the Scaean Gate, waiting to catch sight of the main body of our army. Mother was behind us, supported by her ladies.

Just before midday Achilles made his appearance. He was chasing the Trojan army, all those whose legs could carry them, toward the gate. His new armor, said to have been forged in a single night by the smith god Hephaestus, flashed like the morning star.

Polyxena spotted him; her face revealed the same panic I'd seen that day at the pool. Laodice, white-faced beside her, kept glancing at her sister and then back to Achilles. Something in their manner made me certain Helen had spoken to them about her marriage plan.

"Open the gates," Father told the guards. "But stand ready to close them as soon as our men are safe inside. I fear this madman will try to follow."

It made no sense for Achilles to come near our gates, flanked as they were by champion archers on either side of the high terrace, or to risk being surrounded by Trojans inside our walls. But all of us who watched on that day believed him capable of ripping the massive gates from their hinges and killing every one of us.

The guards released the bolts and pushed back the gates as the first of our soldiers dashed inside. Meanwhile, two of Antenor's sons lured Achilles up into the snaking foothill paths, so that the rest of our army was allowed to retreat inside the gates. For a while he disappeared from our view.

Elderly parents frantic to find their sons had to be pushed back to make room for the routed warriors, who huddled together babbling their stories and drinking water. Our men had no spirit left to look for the missing or seek out their wives and families.

After all had passed through, the guards slammed the great portals and bolted them shut. But one Trojan stayed outside, waiting for his fate to overtake him. His back to the city, he stood gazing up at the rounded hilltop where we had last seen Achilles. This was my brother Hector.

Father begged him to come inside. "Have pity on the men and women of our city. Without your leadership we will all perish."

Hector didn't answer. He faced the mountains, still as a statue.

Mother leaned over the rampart, weeping. "The man's flesh can't be cut!" she cried.

"Achilles is stronger than any man alive," one of her ladies called out.

Another shouted, "He's born of the immortals!"

Helenus joined our parents at the ledge and spoke earnestly, "Hear me, brother! No one will accuse you of cowardice if you refuse this contest."

Hector looked up for the first time, shielding his eyes from the sun. "What would you have me do? Lay down my spear and offer him Helen and all her wealth? Do you think there's the slightest chance he would accept?"

Paris was not there to protest this offer; both he and Helen had wisely stayed off the walls.

"Come, let us open the gates. Achilles can't follow you inside," Helenus urged.

"What of tomorrow and the next day and the day after that?" Hector asked wearily. "Do *you* see a future for me, my brother? Should I strip off this armor—*Achilles' armor*—and let him cut me down like a woman?"

Helenus was weeping, unashamed.

"Zeus Almighty, protect us!" Mother screamed. *"There he is!"*

She pointed to where Achilles was racing down from the hills like a prize stallion gallops over the plain. Even Hector trembled at the sight.

"Hurry, go tell Andromache!" Helenus called out to me.

Andromache! I had forgotten all about her! As I ran toward Hector's mansion, I wondered if she knew what was happening, if she had pleaded with her husband to stay at home.

I found her working at her loom, embroidering a border into a length of purple linen. For a moment I stood in the doorway, amazed at how ordinary the scene looked, how domestic.

"Oh, Cassandra, it's you," she said. "Why must you creep up on people?" She smiled then and beckoned to me. "Come look at this new design, starflowers and anemones. Won't it make a lovely cape?"

Andromache was not usually eager for my company, especially lately. I sat beside her and murmured an appropriate compliment, all the while asking myself why she was here embroidering starflowers while Achilles was outside our walls, hunting down the murderer of his dearest companion.

She brushed a lock of hair from her forehead and bent over her work. I studied her clean profile, the blue shadows underneath her eyes, the pallor of her skin, and I began to understand why she was not up on the walls. She must have decided to deny what was happening out there, to deny everything that was happening to us and concentrate on something she could control.

Poor soul, why shouldn't she want to pretend none of it was real? That her husband was not doomed to die at the hands of a man protected by more powerful gods? That her baby's life was not in danger?

I no longer found her a silly woman. Instead, I felt a stifling tenderness as I watched her embroider. My throat ached with unshed tears. She would probably end up as a slave for some Greek king, drawing water at the well for a queen who would hate her for her delicate features and sweet disposition.

Perhaps *I* could have prevented all this, if I had supported Helen's plan, if I had persuaded Polyxena to sacrifice herself to save her brother, her city. I dropped my head into my hands, no longer capable of weighing the choices.

"Look, I'm using a double knot for the centers," she said. "I still have some of the gold thread from Crete. We've run out of everything else."

I got up and stood behind her, my hand on her shoulder. She flashed me a look of surprise—I was not known for being physically affectionate—and then went on with her stitching.

I didn't tell her about the duel taking place outside our walls. I stood there only minutes, watching her slender fingers twist the gold into knots, but it seemed a very long time.

"Go put on a cauldron of water for Lord Hector's bath," she finally called out to her servants. "He'll want one as soon as he comes in. And Athira, mix some wine for him. The best jar, over there in the corner."

It was then that we heard the first wails of mourning.

CHAPTER FIFTEEN

❧

A s we watched from the walls, Achilles cut holes just above my brother's heels. These he threaded with leather thongs, which he attached to his chariot. For the next twelve days he dragged the body in great circles around Patroclus's tomb and around our walls, smiling his thin-lipped smile up at our family.

It was the scene from my vision, Hector's dark hair caked with blood, his face and outstretched arms cutting grooves in the dust. Only my eyes watched; the rest of me was someplace else. Andromache fainted, was revived, and fainted again and again. Father tore out his hair in tufts that the wind carried out across the plain. Mother tore at her flesh with both hands. Deiphobus punched the wall until the bricks were red with his blood.

Paris kept off the walls, but Helen stayed beside me, tears flowing down her cheeks.

"I know what you're thinking," I snapped. "That Polyxena could have saved him. You've spoken to her. What did she say?"

"Nothing." Helen nodded at Polyxena, whose lovely face

was contorted in pain. "She doesn't know she has the power to change destiny."

"Immortal gods, it's *too late* to change our destiny, too late for your marriage schemes! Can't you understand that?"

"You're wrong, Cassandra! Look at her! You're always talking about the powerlessness of our sex. Polyxena has more power than the whole Trojan army!"

"She would never allow *him* to touch her."

Helen shot me a pitying look. "You're wrong about that too," she said.

We were both wrong about Polyxena. My sister was willing, after all, to let Achilles touch her, but her plans never included marriage.

For more than a week we watched Achilles circling our walls. We went without sleep and took little nourishment. Father moaned and uttered senseless threats, throwing himself into dung heaps and tearing out his hair. It was all we could do to keep him from jumping to his death from the walls or rushing down to the field to attack Achilles himself.

Then, on the evening of the twelfth day after Hector's death, he announced that he would go alone to the Greek camp to ransom his son's body. Hearing this news from the servants, I found him in the main courtyard loading a mule wagon with gold nuggets and a magnificent silver goblet he'd received from my suitor Othronus.

My brothers were there, looking as if they didn't know whether to help him or talk him out of this plan. My mother, face drawn, hair disheveled, was pulling on his arm. "Would you provide another body for this monster, this *cannibal,* to desecrate before our eyes?" she was shouting when I arrived.

At first Father looked as if he didn't recognize his own wife, then his eyes seemed to focus on her. "I've had a dream," he said in a toneless voice. "The god Hermes told me I must approach Achilles myself."

"How can you think of going down there! You used to be famous for your good sense!"

"Hold your tongue, woman! I heard the god's voice with my own ears."

"At least take your personal guards!"

"No warriors. They would only provoke a fight."

"Take *me,* father," said Polyxena, stepping forward from the shade of the gallery, the folds of her white robe shimmering in the slanted sunshine.

"No!" I cried out.

"Achilles would not murder you in my sight," Polyxena said, refusing to look at me.

I saw from my mother's expression that this offer appealed to her. No doubt she'd heard rumors of Achilles' interest in Polyxena; perhaps she'd heard the whole story of Helen's scheming. It was impossible to keep secrets inside the women's quarters.

As my brothers stood mumbling among themselves, I caught Polyxena's eye, and her expression shocked me. Polyxena had always been the gentlest of all the princesses. Now there was a fierce glow in her eyes that warned me not to interfere.

"Let me help," she said to Father. "I'll go get the silver-embroidered robes Paris brought from Sidon."

Father looked from Polyxena to his surviving sons, Paris,

Deiphobus, and Helenus. "Worthless sons! Your sister shows more courage than any of you! At least you can help load the wagon. Polyxena and I will leave before dark."

I caught up with Helenus on his first trip back from the storeroom. "We can't let Polyxena go with him!" I said. Running to keep pace, I sketched a history of Helen's matchmaking efforts. "Helen would still have us marry her to Achilles," I finished breathlessly. "But it's too late for such deals."

"We're still making deals." Helenus hefted a bronze cauldron onto the cart and turned to me. "It may be too late for marriage. But Polyxena's presence may soften his fierce heart."

"There'd be no one to protect her!"

"She's a grown woman, like you. She refuses to stand by and watch our brother being dragged through the dirt. But unlike the rest of us, there may be something *she* can do."

"You've heard of this. From Helen."

He nodded.

"And you approve?"

He snorted in frustration. "It's not up to me to approve or disapprove!"

"She's so young. She doesn't understand the danger. . . ."

"Leave it alone." He pushed me toward the doorway. "Go get some rest. You can barely stand up."

I stood shaking my head as he trudged back to the storeroom. Even my dearest companion had become a stranger.

At twilight, an hour after Achilles' final circle of our walls, we watched them start off across the plain, Father, Polyxena, with a herald driving the mules. Polyxena sat between them, wearing her finest white robe, her face composed, like a temple maiden's.

As they passed through the city, people followed, throwing flowers and weeping as if they were going to their deaths. After they had ridden out of sight, the women went to offer sacrifices at Hermes' temple. Helenus left to get drunk. A yellow moon came up over the rippled plain.

All night I stood atop the Scaean Gate, waiting for their mule cart to return. Just after dawn I spotted the cart and the draped body in its bed. I called out to summon the palace crier.

When they saw Andromache, the crowd around the wagon silently opened a path for her. Her dark hair was tangled in knots. She was still wearing the yellow robe she'd had on the afternoon her husband was killed, when she sat at her loom embroidering starflowers and I stood behind her.

She leaned over the body and wrapped her arms around her husband's shoulders, lifting him toward her. "Look, Cassandra," she said, pushing aside the herald, who wanted to lead her away. "The gods have preserved him. He looks as if he's been dead hours instead of days."

This was true. There was no sign of decay. The body was wrapped in clean linen; blood and dirt had been washed off. I wondered what had prompted such tenderness on the part of Achilles.

"How beautiful he looks," she said, stroking his hair.

"Andromache, we must go prepare the bier."

She began to sob. "I never heard his last words. Never closed his eyes."

It took us an hour to bring her inside and convince the townspeople to allow the wagon to pass into the citadel. Mourners filled the main courtyard, weeping and wailing as the women of the family anointed him, wrapped him in a purple-bordered robe, and placed a wreath of myrtle on his head.

Later a chorus of women chanted the dirge as Troy's citizens filed past the bier, offering farewell messages. When it was Helen's turn, she called Hector the best of all brothers. She stood looking at him, tears running down her cheeks, pale hair falling over her face.

"In all the time I've been here," she said, touching his hand, "I never heard a single unkind word from you. If anyone reproached me for the troubles I brought to your nation, you would always stop them. I weep for you, my dear friend and protector—and for myself."

Achilles would allow us ten days of truce—time to mourn Hector properly and gather wood from the mountains for the funeral rites, so that my brother's soul would not wander endlessly, unable to enter the Land of the Dead. This willingness to allow a proper funeral surprised us, but Father had no explanation for the Greek's change of heart. Since his return with Hector's body Father seemed years older, and somehow detached from the world of men.

We all knew he had loved Hector best. Now he sat beside his son's bier as if turned to stone. Polyxena also refused to speak of Achilles, except to say that he had accepted the ransom and behaved with nobility.

After the burning of the body and the raising of a great mound over the bones we began the games and ritual feasting in Hector's honor, though with our shortages we could hardly call it a feast. Just as Helenus had predicted, we were coming dangerously close to the end of our grain supplies.

On the third day I was supervising the kitchen servants when Laodice came to find me. "Polyxena will take no food or drink," she said.

I passed a tray of bread and cheese to a servant. "We'll make do with this," I said. "We can't spare any more of the barley, and there's no more olive oil in the city. And mind you, see that the slaves refill the water for the mourners' libations as they leave the house of the dead." I shook my head at Laodice. "She'll say nothing to *me*."

"Please come. I'm afraid for her."

I was tired beyond feeling, but I followed her to the women's quarters. We found Polyxena on a couch beside the window, staring out at a gray sky above orange rooftops. Undeserved anger overcame my pity. "What did you have to do to get the body?" I demanded.

"It doesn't matter," she said without looking at us.

"Did Achilles speak of marriage?" Laodice asked.

Polyxena met my eyes with unflinching directness. "He said he would prefer a live daughter to all the gold in Troy. Father pretended not to hear." She shrugged. "Perhaps he didn't hear. He had drunk Achilles' wine after so many days without food."

"Father broke bread with the Greeks?"

She nodded slowly. "They ate together, the two enemies, and then stared at each other a long time in the lamplight. Father fell asleep then, and Achilles talked to me about his own father. He doesn't know if he's dead or alive. . . . I think he expected *us* to feel sorry for *him*."

"Father *fell asleep* in Achilles' tent?" Laodice breathed.

"On one of the cots." Polyxena turned back to the window.

"Did he speak of marriage?" I insisted.

She laughed bitterly. "There will be no marriage," she said, her laughter turning to tears.

I was able to get her to eat a little bread, but it did no good to continue the questioning. She wasn't going to tell us any more about that night in Achilles' tent.

CHAPTER SIXTEEN

❧

J ust as the oracles had predicted, Achilles had little time to savor his victory. On the third day after fighting resumed, Paris killed him with an arrow that entered his flesh just above the heel, below the protection of his silver greaves. Even fatally wounded, Achilles roared at the Trojans to come within spear's reach. Paris and his men stood apart, like peasants watching the death throws of a lion felled in the hunt.

The arrow had nearly amputated his foot, and he bled to death within the hour, despite the frenzied efforts of their surgeon. Down in the Greek camp the mourning lasted for seventeen days.

This truce should have allowed us to gather food and medicine in the mountains. This long-awaited death should have been a rallying point for our people. Instead, our streets were silent; Trojans went on using up our meager grain stores without bothering about the future. Father seemed disinterested in the war, in the impending famine, in who lived and who died.

Of course, Deiphobus fumed because the glory of

Achilles' death had not been his, but no one paid much attention.

"Achilles' fate was to die soon after he killed Hector," Helenus explained wearily. "Does it matter who released the arrow?"

But there was more to this death than even Helenus knew, and Polyxena held the secret.

She had continued to keep to herself. Still, there are few places to hide in a citadel under siege. I found her in what was left of the kitchen garden, filling a basket with the stunted chrysanthemums that remained. These we needed to adorn Hector's tomb. She glanced at me sideways and quickly lowered her eyes.

"Achilles told you the secret of his invulnerability," I said, standing over her. "While Father slept."

"What difference does it make? He's dead. Hector is dead. After this truce more will be dead . . . until it's over."

I knelt beside her and helped pick the yellow flowers, which smelled of autumn afternoons before Helen, before the war. "I suppose you're right. Nobody seems to care."

"*You* still care," Polyxena said, shaking her head.

"I envy them their numbness."

"I was the only one he ever told," she said after a silence. She set down her basket and moved closer. "Even Patroclus didn't know there was a spot on Achilles' body that could be pierced by weapons, just like the flesh of ordinary men."

"His right heel!"

She nodded. "That's where his mother held him when she dipped him in the river Styx to make him invulnerable."

"Why Paris?"

"You think it should have been Helenus who killed him," she said accusingly. "But I told Paris the secret. Only Paris! I wanted Achilles destroyed by Troy's least glorious son, a man ridiculed by his own brothers. I wanted Achilles to know that dishonor in the last seconds of his life—and to know I was the one who betrayed him."

I studied her face, set in hatred, and decided not to press her for what she had done to earn that secret. I imagined the revenge the Greeks would take if they knew, and a thrill of fear coursed through me.

"Weren't you afraid?"

"I was, yes," she said slowly. "There's something quite terrible about him." She crushed a chrysanthemum blossom and opened her hand, releasing its spicy perfume into the still air. "But I don't feel anything anymore."

That was the mood of our city for the next month. No matter what happened on the battlefield, people's reactions were muted. Men no longer called out to one another as they left the gates. Women no longer gathered to watch the fighting. It was as if they were all acting out a destiny written centuries before and wanted to get to the conclusion without further pain, as if they had used up their capacity for pain. Even I stopped going to the walls.

Then one morning I was in the women's quarters supervising the servants at the looms and watching Laodice distractedly tossing the knucklebones. All of a sudden we heard shrieks coming from the main court. I was halfway down the stairs before I realized it was Helen's voice and that she was screaming in Greek, a language she never used anymore.

We found her kneeling in the courtyard, holding Paris in her arms, surrounded by a dozen of his foot soldiers. A bloody cloth was wrapped around his hips, an arrow lay beside him in a pool of blood on the marble floor. The arrow had entered his body just above his groin. He eyes were closed, his face bone white. Helen kept kissing his lips.

"His lips are warm," she told me with an imploring look. "Cassandra, *do* something! You know the sacred herbs!"

One of the men looked at me and shook his head. I knelt beside my brother and placed my ear on his chest. "Helen, I'm sorry. . . . He's dead," I said. "He must have bled to death. . . ."

"No!" she screamed, pushing me away. "You're *lying*!"

Even the men couldn't detach her hold on the body. After she screamed herself hoarse, I got her to take some wine. I'd put a double dose of sleeping powder into it, but she went on wailing for another hour—with no sound coming out of her mouth—before the drug finally took effect. Only then could we remove Paris's corpse from her grip.

After Helen awoke from a day and a half of drugged sleep, it seemed as if her soul had left her body. She didn't weep as we poured the final libations and went through the motions of a cremation ritual. There was no dirge, no farewell speeches. Laodice and Polyxena stayed beside her, but grieving with a sorrow beyond words, she didn't seem to notice their presence. I was not sorry this brother was dead, but it broke my heart to look at her.

The day after the funeral Deiphobus announced that Helen belonged to him now. Father did nothing to intervene, and Helen went along with him to his apartment without a word of protest. I begged Helenus to help her, but he just shrugged.

"We're acting like barbarians!" I shouted at him as he paced the floor. "What will the Greeks think of us?"

"Women have always been pawns of war," he said, "even in Greece."

"Hector would have protected her!"

He glared at me over his shoulder. "But I'm not Hector. I see the future, Cassandra, but I haven't been very successful at changing it."

"What about free will? What about that one chance the gods hold out to us? *What about that?*"

He turned and walked away. He hid from me then, sleeping with his men in the temporary camp outside the walls.

Of course I was helpless to protect her, and Helen had lost all will to protect herself. It didn't seem to matter who shared her bed. We heard no more of her lilting laughter. She stayed in Deiphobus's rooms, with hair uncombed and clothes unwashed, and deep blue circles under her eyes. After the first few days none of us, not even Laodice, went to see her.

And then one morning this mood of national doom lifted, like a rain cloud suddenly dissolved in the midday sun. Just before dawn the town crier roused us with the astounding news that the Greeks had left our shores, all of them.

I climbed to the top of the gate along with women hurriedly adjusting their robes and dragging children behind them. A crowd was already there, shivering in the pink dawn, looking down at an empty plain and beyond it, a harbor empty of Greek ships.

And in the center of the field where our armies once clashed stood the gigantic statue of a horse, almost as tall as our walls, its burnished wood glowing in the morning light. Our scouts returned with the news that the Greek camp was truly deserted, and we poured forth from the gates to examine it.

CHAPTER SEVENTEEN

❦

"Cassandra! Over here!" Laodice called out to me. Deiphobus and two other warriors had scaled the great horse's carved mane and were waving down at the crowd. Even Polyxena was there. It was wonderful to see her laughing up at them.

"It's an offering to Athena," Laodice said when I joined them. "We know all about it from one of their men."

"His name is Sinon," Polyxena added. "He hid during the evacuation because he overheard Odysseus plotting to kill him as soon as they set sail. Some sort of gambling quarrel. . . ."

"I know what he's saying," I said. "I've just been listening to Helenus question the man. His story doesn't make sense. I think he's lying."

But my sisters were too excited to listen. "They made the horse too wide for our gates," Laodice interrupted, "so that we couldn't take it into our city!"

"Sinon says it will bring prosperity to whoever owns it," Polyxena cried.

"Then why didn't they build it in sections and take it home with them when they sailed?" I asked, stepping back to study the construction, shading my eyes from the blazing sun. "They *have* built it in sections!"

"Why must you question everything?" said Laodice. "Even the gods' blessings?"

"Because it doesn't make sense for the Greeks to give us something that would bring prosperity. Why should they leave a parting gift? They despise us."

But I didn't want to argue the point. With the sun directly overhead I was beginning to feel dizzy. "Has Helen been here?" I asked.

Laodice shook her head. "She won't leave her rooms. Even now. Maybe if you talked to her? Cassandra—are you all right?"

My legs began to tremble; two darts of pain struck the back of my neck. The sun blazed. The field rippled and then grew darker, until I was inside the vision from my dream, surrounded by the writhing bodies of our warriors. But the setting was no longer the battlefield. It was the streets of Troy that ran with our mens' blood, and the great horse towered over the destruction.

"It's a trick!" I shouted. *"Set fire to it!"* Stumbling, I started toward the gate. Laodice caught up and supported me. "I have to find Helenus," I insisted, my head throbbing with pain.

"Sit here," she said, "on this patch of grass."

Polyxena came running with a cup of water; a house servant arrived to stand over me with a sunscreen. In a daze I watched Deiphobus and a crowd of men lift the horse onto rollers. Other men were knocking down a section of the wall with stone hammers, enlarging the Scaean Gate so that they could pull the great horse into our city.

This time I wasn't alone in my warning. As I sat there, overwhelmed by my own helplessness, a priest named Laocoön shouted at them to wheel the horse into the sea, that it would bring disaster. He even managed to throw a spear into its wooden belly before Deiphobus's men came and dragged him away.

It was useless to try to reason with the mob. They would never believe me. I had to find Helenus! They might listen to *him*. I started forward, swaying on my feet, and collapsed into a heap on the grass.

I didn't find my twin until late afternoon.

They had dragged the huge horse into the outer bailey. Someone had draped a chain of laurel around its neck. I stood gazing up at it, trying to decipher its secret. I had just awakened from the sleep of death that often followed my visions.

All over the citadel people were feasting, dancing, and singing. Surrounded by my countrymen, by their circling dances and shrieking laughter, deafened by the drunken singing, the flutes and pipes, I was more alone than I had ever been.

Deiphobus came staggering by, singing a sea chantey. Through the open portals of the men's court I could see female house servants neglecting their duties to join a line dance with some foot soldiers, who stopped to refill their cups each time they passed the wine jar in the corner.

At the hearth altar servants were roasting an ox that had been sacrificed that afternoon in gratitude for the great gift. The smell of burning fat filled the air. I had eaten nothing all day, and tasted no meat in months. I felt so light-headed, it was difficult to take in what was happening around me, but it seemed for a moment that howls of pain and groans of dying men were superimposed on the shouts of merriment.

I turned back to the horse and saw the fire reflected in its polished flanks. There was a sickness in my stomach, a pounding in my ears. As if moving in a dream, I ran to the fire and grabbed one of the logs by the end that hadn't yet caught the flames, dragging it toward the great horse.

No one was going to listen to my warnings. But I could take advantage of the confusion to set fire to the menace myself.

Deiphobus must have seen me, because he came at me from behind, hitting me with the force of his body and knocking me to the ground. Muttering curses, he kicked the burning wood away from the horse.

"Crazy woman!" he screamed. "How long must we endure your ravings? You would destroy a gift from the immortals?"

"You're eating your last food!" I shouted back. "You're already starting down a road used by ghosts."

"Go make your predictions to the Greeks!" He would have struck me, but suddenly Helenus was between us, kneeling beside me, gathering me into his arms.

Deiphobus shook his fist at us and then stumbled away.

"You can do what he suggests," Helenus said into my ear. "There are twenty Greek warriors hiding inside." He nodded at the retreating Deiphobus. "Twenty is all they'll need."

I could make no sense of his words.

"Twenty Greek warriors are inside the *horse*," he repeated slowly. "Odysseus and Menelaus, Agamemnon, Ajax. . . ."

"Have you too seen a vision?"

"Not just a vision. I have an exact picture of the compartment inside, which is lined with benches, and the secret door inside the saddle."

I sat shaking my head, like a person suddenly roused from the deepest sleep.

"The wooden horse was my own design. I showed them how to build it."

"But *why*?"

He took my hand, which felt numb in the grip of his larger one, and pulled me to my feet. "We need a quiet place to talk."

"Immortal gods, what treachery is this?" I breathed.

But he just dragged me after him.

We climbed the hill to the temple sanctuaries and sat down outside Apollo's temple to catch our breath. It wouldn't have mattered which temple he chose; they were all empty. In contrast to the city it was peaceful up on the hill. The faint drumming from down below was punctuated by the chirping of birds. An occasional burst of laughter floated up to us. The side I had fallen on ached, and my right leg was bleeding. Distractedly, I blotted the blood with the corner of my robe. I could still hear the pounding of my heart in my ears. *"Why would you help the Greeks?"*

"Look, our people have abandoned their gods." Helenus laughed bitterly. "Even the priests are down there."

From where we sat, we could see ant-sized revelers celebrating this sudden release from seven years of war.

"Tell me about the horse!" I urged.

"The horse was an act of mercy on my part," he began.

I turned toward him with a gasp of protest, and he put

up a hand to silence me. "We'll all be starving to death before winter. Better that Troy dies all at once."

"*No!*"

"A sudden, merciful death instead of a lingering one."

"Then there's no chance for us?" I said after a silence. My voice sounded as if it were coming from far away.

He shook his head slowly. "Whatever his reasons, Zeus has withdrawn his support."

"He's a monster! They're all monsters," I said, glancing fearfully over my shoulder at Apollo's abandoned temple.

Helenus nodded. "The gods sit on Olympus enjoying our struggles to survive. . . . But we can still surprise them."

I felt hollow with fear and bewilderment.

"We can't escape our destruction. But we can choose *how* we will perish. . . . I have chosen for us."

He leaned back against a column and closed his eyes. "The Greeks were willing to cooperate because it suited their plans. Remember that day you saw me outside the walls, with Odysseus? The day we burned our dead? The two of us were negotiating a bargain. I offered an end to the seven-year standoff. . . ."

"In exchange for what?"

"In exchange for you, Cassandra." He sighed. "And for my own miserable life."

He opened his eyes then, his face twisted in pain. I reached to touch his cheek, not wanting to hear the rest of his confession.

"The Greeks think highly of my gift of sight," he said. "I simply told them what they needed to do to finish us off. The old prophecies are quite specific." He nodded down at the citadel, where the mane of the huge horse projected above the roof tiles. "They've only pretended to sail away. The Greek fleet is hiding behind the island."

I frowned out at the island of Tenedos, silhouetted against a blazing sunset. "What about the girls, Polyxena and—?"

"The enemy won't even need to break down the Scaean Gate. Our people have done it for them. By the time the main body of their army gets here, the warriors inside the horse will have killed off Deiphobus and the others. There's a hidden latch. At the corner of the saddle."

What about Laodice and Polyxena?

"I couldn't negotiate their release. The Greek kings have all staked claims on our women. Except Odysseus . . ."

"I can't leave my sisters to face this alone!"

"You won't have to." He dropped his head into his hands, and I could barely hear his next words. "Odysseus thought he had worked out all the details. . . . But Agamemnon has gone back on his word."

Helenus raised his head and turned to look at me. Tears ran freely down his cheeks. "Agamemnon is refusing to let you go."

I didn't understand right away. Not until I saw the fear in his eyes. "*Me?* I'm to be *his* prize?"

"He probably thinks you should feel honored," Helenus said with a choking laugh.

Agamemnon, who let them kill his own daughter? I sat shaking my head, wanting to die.

"You've never even noticed him fighting his duels right below the gate where you stood," Helenus was saying as if from a great distance. "He's been trying to get your attention for years."

I could no longer hear my brother's words, only the

~ 178 ~

pounding in my ears. I looked stupidly down at the harbor and then up into the mountains, searching for an escape route. How amazingly tranquil the world looked in the slanting sunlight. My stomach churned. For a moment I thought I was going to vomit.

"But he won't have you! Cassandra, listen to me!" Helenus was holding me by the shoulders. "I can kill him before the others get me! *Agamemnon will never have you!*"

I leaned into his chest. His tears wet my cheeks, mingling with my own. After a while I was able to get my breath, and then to breathe deeply to calm myself.

Down on the horizon an orange sun slipped into turquoise sea. I listened to Helenus's heartbeat, wondering if this were the last time we would ever hold each other. How would I go on living without him?

"What good would it do?" I finally said. "If you kill Agamemnon, I would only be handed over to another one." I pulled away and looked up at his face. "You've seen this before, haven't you? *Us* at the Temple of Apollo watching the sun set? You telling me of my destiny?"

I could always read the truth in my brother's eyes. "And what have you seen for yourself? *Tell* me!" When he remained speechless, I said, "I've always known you would survive this war."

He flinched as though I had struck him. "Yes, I will *live*!" His whole body shook with sobs. "My father slaughtered. All my brothers. My mother insane. My sisters house slaves of Greek kings. . . . *And I will live!*"

I held him tight until his grief was spent. "Is it still arranged for you to leave the city before they attack?" I asked then.

"I was to be down at the harbor an hour after nightfall. They've arranged my passage with some horse traders. Odysseus was being kind. He didn't want me to have to watch." He stroked my hair. "Oh, Cassandra. I've been over every possible escape plan. Even if I could find a crew, the Greeks would be after us as soon as we rounded Tenedos. There's no hope."

"Listen to me, Helenus. There's still hope. That's why you must live—Wait, listen!" I took his face between my hands. "Just knowing you are safe—somewhere—will give us hope."

He shook his head, his thick lashes wet with tears. I had never loved him more.

"As long as you're alive, you'll be working to free us, buy us back! Perhaps with Odysseus's help? He's a good man; you respect him." I didn't wait for an answer. "Laodice and Polyxena! We have to bring them up here, to the Temple of Athena. The Greeks won't harm us in the sanctuary of their own patron goddess. And Helen? What do you see for her?"

"I've had no visions. Odysseus thinks Menelaus will kill her."

"Then we'll have to change his mind."

"Don't distract me; I won't leave here without you, Cassandra."

"But you *will*! If you die fighting for me—a useless fight—you'll leave me forever!"

We looked at each other a long time. "Please!" I reached for his hands. "I'm trying to be brave. Help me. If you love me, you'll decide to live. You'll start a new city. A new Troy."

The sky had darkened from mauve to violet; the great shadow of the temple stretched out to cover us.

"How long do we have?" I breathed.

"An hour. Maybe two."

"Then we must hurry. You can bring the girls up here to Athena's temple and then leave from here for the harbor. I'll run and find Helen. I'll explain what she has to do."

"My wonderful Cassandra. Always a plan."

I smiled, my eyes filling with fresh tears. I didn't have a plan. I had no idea what I would say to Helen. I had jumped desperately into activity because I didn't dare think about Agamemnon. And because I knew that if I lingered there with Helenus, I would never have the courage to let him go.

My brother had to be down at the harbor an hour after nightfall to meet the Greeks, and I was going to make sure he got there on time.

CHAPTER EIGHTEEN

❦

B y the time I made it down to the city, dusk had set-
tled into the walkways; servants were lighting pine
torches in the men's hall. I looked for Deiphobus—
he was still drinking with his men, holding a full goblet in
both hands—then ran up the stairs to his apartment on the
far side of the hall.

Helen was asleep. Since Paris's death she had spent most
of her time in bed. I had to shake her awake. She blinked at
me with frightened eyes, then groaned and struggled to pull
away.

"The Greeks are inside our walls!" I hissed. "Their ships
haven't sailed for home!"

"Go away."

"Their warriors are inside the horse!"

She pushed hair out of her eyes. "The . . . horse . . . ?
How could they?"

"There's no time to explain. Just believe me. Menelaus is
in there! He'll come here as soon as our men fall asleep!"

"Paris is dead; he can't kill him again. Go away and let
me sleep."

"*You* are here! Odysseus thinks your husband will take his revenge on *you*."

Her eyes widened. She stopped struggling.

"Will Deiphobus come back here?"

"Yes, always," she said with a grimace.

"As soon as he passes out, you'll have to hide his weapons. Listen to me! Menelaus has to think you're on his side."

She began to weep, not bothering to wipe her tears. "He'll never believe that," she sobbed. "He'll throw me from the walls. The Trojan women will be happy to see me die."

"You can change his mind."

"He hates me. They all hate me!"

"You told me Aphrodite had promised you to Paris, that you were powerless to resist the goddess. Remember?"

"I wish I had died before . . ."

"*No more wishing!* It's *done!* You left Menelaus to follow Paris! Paris is *dead*; you can't ever bring him back. But you can live! To be a mother to your daughter."

"Hermione! She's thirteen now, the same age I was when I met Menelaus."

I smoothed a lock of hair out of her eyes. "Don't you want to see her again?" I asked gently. Her hair was lank and oily, her tunic filthy. "We've got to find you a clean robe. Where are your servants?"

She surveyed the room with a dazed expression. "Gone off."

"Menelaus has to be captivated by your beauty. Like the first day he saw you. I can braid silver ropes into your hair. We'll put alkanet juice on your cheeks and some kohl on your eyebrows."

"Cassandra." She touched my cheek. "You're not any

good at braiding hair . . . and you don't approve of alkanet juice. Cassandra, you're crying!"

We wept together then, holding tight to each other. Her shoulder blades were sharp, and instead of her usual rosepetal perfume, she smelled of the odors I associated with house slaves.

"How will I get by without you?" she said. Then, with sudden fear in her eyes, "What will happen to you?"

I shook my head.

"You *know*, don't you?"

"The Greek kings have made their selections. Agamemnon is to have me."

"*Immortal gods!*"

I bit my lip to stop the tears. "I still have time to face my destiny. There's no time left for you; Deiphobus could return any moment. I'll heat water for your bath. Can you find something clean to wear?"

Helen was right. I made a mess of the braid. I was never skilled at such tasks. Now my trembling fingers would not behave at all. I kept imagining the creak of hidden panels, the muffled cries from the first throats being slit. Once in a while a burst of drunken laughter floated up from the men's hall, but there were ever-longer patches of silence. The celebration was winding down. Cursing in frustration, I was combing out my tangled excuse for a plait when Helen's maid Clymene returned home.

She seemed shocked to see her lady out of bed, bathed and dressed in a mauve linen robe with a silver-embroidered hem.

"Here, take over," I said, handing her the comb. "And mind you, be quick about it."

"Don't leave me!" Helen grabbed for my hand.

"I have to meet Polyxena and Laodice up at the temple."

Helen was crying again. I wiped a tear from her cheek. "You'll ruin your makeup," I said. Even with her sharp shoulder blades and the new suffering in the lines around her mouth, her incomparable beauty shone through.

"Will Menelaus ever believe the goddess Aphrodite brought these troubles down upon me?" she asked.

"He won't be able to resist you. There now, wipe your eyes."

"Don't *you* blame me? For all you've lost?"

"I've given up trying to assign blame."

"Agamemnon will admire your courage."

"I don't even have the courage to throw myself from the walls," I said, forcing a smile.

She shook her head. "You've always given me strength, Cassandra."

"And you've given me joy," I said in a choked voice.

My face hurt from the effort of holding my mouth in a brave line. And I would have to go on being brave when I joined my sisters at Athena's temple. Suddenly, I was too tired to pretend. I turned and ran from her.

"Cassandra, *don't leave me!*" she called after me.

I ran out of the palace and down into the garden. I hadn't the strength to climb the hill to take charge of my sisters. I didn't want to have to protect Polyxena from Greek vengeance. I didn't want to face life without my brother Helenus.

I wanted to die.

I dropped down on the warm stones, shedding my tears into the dust. I didn't have to *do* anything, I told myself.

I didn't have to take charge of anybody. I could go back to the outer bailey and wait for the Greeks to come out of the horse, give myself up without a struggle. Or I could stay there on the paving stones until one of them came and stumbled over my body.

The court was deserted, the city hushed, waiting. I don't know if I lay there minutes or hours.

And then, in the darkness, I thought I heard the click of a latch being disengaged. I crept into a kneeling position, listening with every pore, like a runner at the start of a race. The seconds stretched endlessly; a dog barked twice. I was afraid to breathe, and then, so faintly I knew I might be imagining it, I sensed in my body the vibrations of footsteps—male footsteps—moving somewhere in the city.

I jumped to my feet and set off at a run, my breath burning in my throat as I raced up the hill. Fortunately, there was only a sliver of the moon, and I knew every stone of that path to the sanctuaries. A light beckoned from the Temple of Athena, the signal that Polyxena and Laodice were up there, that Helenus had taken the foothill trail to the harbor.

Down below me stretched the dark shape of the sprawling palace. Helen would be outside Deiphobus's apartments, waiting for Menelaus. My parents would be sound asleep, perhaps dreaming of Troy's past glories, of their lost sons in the flush of life. I knew both were longing to join them in the sleep of death. Still, I couldn't bear to thing of their awakening.

And what of poor Andromache and little Astyanax? I imagined them torn from their beds, terrified by blazing torches and screams of the dying, by the choking dust mingled with smoke from the burning city. I knew the Greeks would save their worst revenge for the widow and son of Manslaughtering Hector.

It is strange to tell of the next few seconds, because I was very afraid—more afraid than I'd ever been in my life. But somehow I was also watching myself turn around and retrace my steps down the path toward Hector's mansion.

CHAPTER NINETEEN

❧

ndromache's servants were slumped together in
the entry courtyard. They didn't even stir as I
pushed open the door, which they had left
unbolted. I stopped just inside to listen—no more vibrations, only the servants' rhythmic snoring. Still, I could picture in my mind's eye the scene I would see from the
landing two floors above, which looked out on the outer
bailey where the great horse stood. I ran up the stairs and
hid just inside an open window.

At first I could only make out the horse's huge silhouette.
Then my breath caught in my throat. In the moving glow of
a lantern I saw a ladder propped against the horse's far
side. Two warriors—I couldn't see their faces—steadied it
while a third climbed to the ground. Incapable of moving, I
watched a spear and two swords being carefully lowered
into waiting hands. Then I found myself dashing toward
Andromache's rooms. I had forgotten to remove my sandals.
Their clatter on the tiles screamed into the silence.

The baby's nurse was asleep on the couch next to the
door; Astyanax lay curled in her arms. In the great carved

bed she had once shared with Hector, Andromache looked amazingly peaceful, her hands palm down at her sides.

I knelt and touched her shoulder, ready to clamp my hand over her mouth if she cried out. "Andromache, wake up!" I whispered.

She rolled to her side and opened her eyes. "What's wrong?"

"The Greeks are inside our walls!"

"The Greeks have gone home," she said, glancing over at Astyanax.

"Shhh! They've only pretended to sail away. They're inside the horse. . . ." My words were confirmed by a strangled cry in the darkness. Andromache leaped out of bed and gathered up her son. The nurse groaned in her sleep.

"Leave her. And keep him quiet," I said, nodding at Astyanax, who still slept.

Andromache reached for her lamp.

"No light. And no shoes. Get two of your darkest capes from the wardrobe."

It surprised me that Andromache obeyed without question. We heard rustling in the center court. My hands shook as I removed my sandals. "We'll go up the hill," I whispered. "To the Temple of Athena."

We were edging down the stairs in the darkness when we heard footsteps, the rasp of a sword being removed from its scabbard, and then a terror-stricken voice crying out, *"Zeus, protect me!"*

A beam of light penetrated the stairwell where we cowered. Andromache's eyes were wild with terror. Then we were plunged into darkness. I touched her lips with my fingers and gestured that I was going down to the bottom.

Once there I wrapped the cape around my head and peeked around the door frame.

In the entry court a Greek warrior stood nudging the servants' bodies with his foot. One of the poor souls was writhing pitifully and clutching his entrails with both hands, gasping his final breaths.

I stopped breathing as the Greek—I think it was Lesser Ajax—turned in the direction of the doorway. He was reaching for his torch when a second Greek ran into the court and barked out a command I couldn't understand. Picking up his torch, the first man followed his companion down the gallery toward the main palace.

Another scream of terror rang out from the direction of the men's hall, then a sudden crash, as if a heavy chest had fallen to the floor.

All was black inside the house. I felt my way back to where Andromache waited. "They've killed your guards. We'll have to climb over your roof to the storerooms at the other side—then to the flat roof where they dry the figs. From there we can get down to the kitchen gardens."

When she stayed blocking the stairwell, I gave her a push.

"I *can't* climb out on the roof! I'm *afraid*!" she cried. "We're trapped inside here."

Astyanax stirred and whimpered. "Here, give him to me," I snapped. She only hesitated a second. He was awake, but still the son of a Trojan hero. "Hush now. There's a good boy," I said, and he clung to my neck without a word.

"All right then. We'll take our chances on the ground. We won't have to cut across the entry court to reach the storerooms," I said, thinking out loud. "Just keep to the shadow of the walls. Stay behind me."

"*Cassandra, I can't!*"

"You can't stay here. Think of what the Greeks will do to *you!*"

She raised a fist to her mouth.

"Come on, take my hand," I coaxed.

As Andromache followed me down the stairs, I prayed to all the gods that the baby wouldn't cry out, that the entry court would be empty of Greeks, that they would go first to the main palace with its gold and silver, its noble inhabitants waiting to be murdered—and leave the food stores and kitchens for later.

Hector's mansion formed an angle with the first of the kitchen storehouses, from which we took the stairs to the flat roof. Astyanax was beginning to whine by the time we reached the gardens, but it didn't matter. The clash of weapons and groans of the dying rose from the palace like a deadly chorus to cover any sounds we might have made. Only once did we come close to being caught, when a couple of infantrymen darted down a parallel path. But they were so intent on reaching the main palace that they didn't notice us crouching behind a low wall.

We stayed off the pathway to the temples, scrambling up the rocks instead. Astyanax was so heavy, my whole body ached, but my bleeding feet had ceased to feel any pain. At the lowest shrine I passed him back to his mother and we stopped a moment to look down at our city.

The lights of the Greek fleet sparkled in the harbor. We could see their army pouring through the Scaean Gate in a torchlit procession of triumph. Even if they spotted us, we would reach the temple of their patron goddess before they could. Besides, our conquerors had more pressing matters to occupy them.

They had set fire to the main hall. A second fire was raging in the men's quarters, the blaze lighting up the night sky. Horses and dogs were stampeding in terror through the streets. I imagined I could hear the groans of the men, the wailing of the women.

I thought of my mother and father and shuddered. My mother's gray hair would protect her from rape, and she was worth more alive, as a slave to some Greek king. There was no hope for my father, only that he would be allowed to die quickly, a death, a forgetfulness, he longed for.

Then I imagined Helen throwing herself at Menelaus's feet, and her husband looking down at her and dropping his sword. Helen would become a powerful ally for us, I told myself. And wherever we were taken in the Greek lands, my brother Helenus would be working to arrange our ransoms. He was well respected, even by the enemy.

There was hope, at least for some of us. Someday we might be reunited, a community of Trojan women, keeping our memories and our traditions.

The light from the Temple of Athena beckoned us on. Polyxena and Laodice were up there; perhaps they had already spotted us on the trail.

Down below, Troy was dying. For reasons we would never understand, our great city had outlived its destiny. But some of us—four women and a baby—would be awake to meet our new masters. And we would stand together, holding one another's hands and wiping one another's tears.

AUTHOR'S EPILOGUE

For Helen of Troy, at least, I can offer readers a happy ending. In the ancient sources for these well-loved stories a string of authors took up her defense. In their retellings Helen was able to convince Menelaus that he shouldn't throw her from the walls, that none of her actions were her fault, that she could not have escaped the fate of loving Paris. Menelaus brought her home to Sparta, where she was reunited with her daughter and lived a long and happy life. The gods allowed her to keep her beauty well into old age. She enjoyed playing hostess to heroes from the great war, who liked to gather and talk about old times.

Not all the Greek kings managed to visit her in Sparta, however. Some had angered gods who got even during the voyage home across dangerous seas. It took Odysseus ten years to sail back to his wife, Penelope, after the war ended, just as the oracles had predicted. A poem called the *Odyssey* tells of his adventures along the way.

Ancient authors provided some happy endings for the defeated Trojans. Helenus escaped and founded a new Troy in a place called Buthrotum. He was on such good terms with the Greeks that he eventually managed to ransom Andromache, with whom he had several children. According to the Roman poet Virgil, another Trojan prince named Aeneas escaped with his father and son and founded the city of Rome.

There is no record anywhere of a reunion of the women who had been trapped together inside Troy's walls during the long siege. In the *Iliad*, the earliest written version of the story of the Trojan War, there was almost no mention of women. (Even Helen, who supposedly caused the whole thing, rates only a few sentences.) We think that the *Iliad* was composed by a poet named Homer around 750 B.C. He sang his story-poems to an audience of Greek noblemen, who were mainly interested in the battles and exploits of other noblemen.

Centuries later another Greek wrote a tragic play called *The Trojan Women*. But in most retellings we hear about the Trojan women only incidentally. Most did not fare very well. Andromache's son, Astyanax, was snatched from her arms during the sack of the city and thrown from the walls. The ghost of Achilles ordered the Greeks to sacrifice Polyxena to avenge his death, threatening to stir up terrible storms during their return home if this execution did not take place immediately. (He was kind enough to allow the Trojans to bury her body.) The gods arranged for poor Laodice to disappear into a cloud of dust or into a gaping hole in the earth, depending on the version.

And what of Cassandra? One source tells of her going mad as she watched the destruction of her beloved city; another has her leading the women in a mass suicide. Some myths show her returning home to Mycenae as

Agamemnon's battle prize and bearing him two sons. Agamemnon was eventually murdered by his wife, Clytemnestra, to avenge the death of her daughter Iphigenia. In some versions of this story Cassandra was murdered along with him. But we also find hints that she may have survived the war to start a new dynasty.

That's the story I like to believe. What attracted me to Cassandra was her unfailing resistance, her willingness to "fight like a tigress" to protect the people she loved, as I have Paris say of her. For me, Cassandra seemed to embody the Greek ideal of a noble life as a continued act of faith, a continued quest for who we are in a universe ruled by powerful forces we can neither understand nor control.

Scholars now believe that a great war *did* take place between the Mycenaean Greeks and the wealthy Trojans across the sea in Asia Minor, probably over trade and control of the entrance to the Black Sea. Still, many early civilizations have stories of beautiful princesses who triggered great wars by running away with handsome enemy princes. I prefer to believe Helen was real and that she was more than just conspicuously beautiful. I like to think she had a kind of innocence, a capacity for joy, that were part of her legendary appeal.

In present-day Turkey the site of a great battle between Bronze Age warriors has been excavated. A brilliant, eccentric German named Heinrich Schliemann believed that the *Iliad* could not have been written in such detail if it had not been historically true. Using Homer's poem as guide and road map, he unearthed a citadel with great towers and encircling walls that many now believe was the real Troy. He also discovered buried treasure—copper cauldrons, silver vases, gold cups, and a collection of ornaments he called "Helen's Jewels." Among the buttons and earrings was a gold diadem like the ones described in my story. It was crafted of ninety strands of leaf and flower pendants, a design unknown in Asia Minor. Schliemann photographed his beautiful Greek wife wearing it. He wanted to believe in Helen too.

Not far from these excavations one enterprising descendent of Priam has built a thirty-foot model of the Trojan horse, in which tourists can have their pictures taken. At his adjoining refreshment stand they can order Cokes and sandwiches. And if they climb to the top of the hill, they'll find ruins of what may have been the Scaean Gate, where women watched the fighting, and above it, the site of the Temple of Athena, where Cassandra took the women to safety at the end of my story.

But in some accounts even this holy place did not offer protection. One source has Cassandra raped by Lesser Ajax right there in the temple, still clinging to the statue of the goddess and crying out for mercy. Later Ajax's hometown of Locris actually had to pay a price for the sins committed by him in the *Iliad*. Starting around 700 B.C. the Locrians began sending a yearly quota of virgins to Athena's temple in Troy, where they were mistreated during their lifelong service to the goddess. This practice went on for more than a thousand years, a testament to the power of these stories over the lives of the people in that ancient world.

And what of these myths today? We're still writing Broadway musicals about Helen's beauty and talking about our *Achilles' heels* (our place of greatest vulnerability). The *Achilles tendon* connects the foot with the leg. A *Cassandra* is someone who foretells a gloomy future and is not believed. Computer hackers use the term *Trojan horse* to describe a computer virus that is introduced into a system disguised as a virus cleaner.

Nothing exists in the old sources about a friendship between Cassandra and Helen. I created that story myself. Still, it seemed entirely possible for these two outcasts to have been drawn together in the way I described. Unlike Homer, singing his poems to an audience of noblemen, I was writing for readers who, like myself, may have wondered about the girls and women who watched the fighting from Troy's walls and waited for their destinies inside the women's quarters.

Throughout the centuries these legends have given birth to new legends, just as a stone thrown into a pool sets off chain reactions of ever-widening circles. And each new generation of storytellers finds new meanings and creates new personalities for these Greeks and Trojans from a bronze-age civilization. I think we'll still be doing it—retelling the story of the Trojan War—when we've established space colonies on Mars.

The myths, after all, are stories of the soul. And as they are reborn in each new age, they continue to teach us about what it means to be alive as human beings—daughters and sisters, fathers and brothers, mothers and children—building families and cities, planting gardens and making war, praying to our gods and mourning our dead.